"My people thank you," said the chief.

Of all the braves, one in particular stood out. Mrs. Clarke identified him as Brother-of-the-Wolf, the same one who raised the dogs. His sleek, muscular physique spoke of the hours he had trained as a hunter.

The last Chippewa Elizabeth vaccinated was Beloved-of-the-Forest. When she finished, the Indian woman hesitated before she left, and spoke to Elizabeth through Mrs. Clarke. "Thank you, daughter of white medicine man. Though it is too late for my child, the kindness you have shown today will save many of my people." She bowed her head and left on quiet moccasins.

After Beloved-of-the-Forest had gone from the lodge, Elizabeth spoke to Mrs. Clarke. "She seems to have changed her attitude about me since this morning, when she wouldn't even let me look at her baby."

Mrs. Clarke nodded. "When I came with her to her father, he impressed upon her how generous your offer was, and how important the vaccinations were. He told her how, in times past, whole tribes had been wiped out by smallpox, and that their village could be destroyed in a few days if it weren't for your help."

ELIZABETH OF SAGINAW BAY

Donna Winters

BOOKS

of the Zondervan Publishing House
Grand Rapids, Michigan

A Note from the Author:
I love to hear from my readers! You may correspond with me by writing:

> Donna Winters
> 1415 Lake Drive S.E.
> Grand Rapids, MI 49506

ELIZABETH OF SAGINAW BAY
Copyright 1986 by Donna Winters

Serenade/Saga is an imprint of Zondervan Publishing House. 1415 Lake Drive, S.E., Grand Rapids, Michigan 49506.

ISBN 0-310-47272-5

Edited by Ann McMath
Designed by Kim Koning

Printed in the United States of America

86 87 88 89 90 91 / 10 9 8 7 6 5 4 3 2 1

To my mother
Frances Patte Rogers

CHAPTER 1

ELIZABETH MORGAN STOOD on the dock facing the untamed eastern bank of the Saginaw River, a few miles south of Saginaw Bay. She searched for signs of civilization. At the dock stood a blockhouse. Sprinkled among the towering white pines were perhaps a half dozen primitive log cabins. Where were the streets, the clapboard houses, the picket fences, and all the other signs of the thriving new town in which she had come to live on this July day in 1837? *Perhaps they're farther back from the river*, she told herself.

Elizabeth pushed a windblown lock of dark brown hair away from her face, then rested her brown eyes on Jacob, her thirty-year-old third-generation-banker husband of less than one month. The late afternoon sunshine highlighted his wavy, golden hair. The strength in his six-foot frame and the spirit of adventure they had shared moments before landing buoyed her confidence. But tiny lines newly appearing at the corners of his blue eyes told her without words that their honeymoon trip into the wilderness had taken a toll on him, too. Elizabeth wondered what troubled him, but knew her question would have to wait.

A middle-aged man, probably Jacob's uncle, hurried down the riverbank to meet them. "Jacob! Good to see you, nephew."

"Uncle Will! I thought we'd never make it, even though Captain Winthrop assured me he knew the location of Riverton." The men hugged. Jacob slipped his arm about Elizabeth and drew her close. "Uncle Will, meet Mrs. Jacob Morgan."

"Mrs. Jacob Morgan, my pleasure." Will kissed her hand. His bushy beard tickled her, making her tired smile grow wider. Uncle Will, in his faded trousers, stained cotton shirt, and dusty boots epitomized her expectations of a backwoodsman rather than the land speculator and banker Jacob claimed his uncle to be.

Elizabeth greeted him warmly. "Uncle Will, I'm pleased to make your acquaintance after all Jacob has told me about you."

"The pleasure is mine, Elizabeth. You're even prettier than Jacob said in his letters. Now follow me and I'll show you to your honeymoon cabin." A mischievous glint lit his eyes.

Split logs embedded into the riverbank provided solid treads on the moderate incline. With Jacob's arm tightly around her waist, Elizabeth picked up her skirts and followed Will. *We'll never be able to afford to build a nice house in this remote corner of the world*, Elizabeth thought as they climbed the sloping bank. *It could take the rest of Jacob's endowment just to hire a good carpenter and ship all the building supplies here.*

Unlike many young couples who began married life with little savings, Jacob had received a generous endowment from his father when he turned thirty, two months before their wedding. Unfortunately, Jacob had already spent a lot of money for their passage and hotel accommodations, insisting on the best for his new bride, despite her desire to conserve their resources. *I have to stop worrying*, Elizabeth thought. *Jacob has too much banking experience to make poor judgments about money.* But worry she did. With their marriage had come changes in her thoughtful and intelligent husband. As if, suddenly, he had to prove to the world how much money he could accumulate—and spend—for his new bride. She sometimes had faint longings for the "old" Jacob.

When they reached the top of the incline, Elizabeth looked around for the town that Uncle Will had described in his letters to Jacob, but still didn't see any white frame houses, or dirt streets. Thick forest surrounded the small clearing, which was dotted with rude cabins and crisscrossed by narrow paths. *Riverton must be nearby*, she assured herself.

A group of settlers had gathered on the riverbank to welcome the new arrivals. Will made brief introductions—the Farrells, the Stones, the Tylers, the Langtons, and the Reverend and Mrs. Clarke. Elizabeth was certain she would forget most of their names, except for Mrs. Langton, whose deeply lined face spoke of hardships and struggles, and Mrs. Clarke, whose kind round face held a peaceful smile.

Elizabeth felt uncomfortable under Mrs. Langton's scrutiny, her critical eye taking stock of the newcomer. Mrs. Clarke stepped beside Elizabeth and squeezed her hand. "Perhaps you could come to my cabin for tea one day soon, dear, after you've had some time to settle in."

"I'd like that. Thank you, Mrs. Clarke," Elizabeth answered, feeling grateful that she would have at least one new friend.

Uncle Will led them to their borrowed cabin. When he swung open the door, a musty odor greeted Elizabeth. "It's not much, but for the two of you, just newly wed and all, I'm sure it'll do. Joseph LaMore built this place last fall and stayed here for a while, but he's gone to Canada for a while. By the time he returns, Jacob, we'll have your place ready."

When she stepped inside, stark walls, though well chinked, met Elizabeth's large brown eyes. Surely she would wake up and realize this place existed only in her dreams. A little light filtered in through the six-paned windows on either side wall. There was little furniture; in one corner stood a rope bed topped with feather ticking. At the back, an open hearth fireplace with an iron crane determined the manner in which Elizabeth would prepare their meals.

For the daughter of a doctor who cared more for learning the latest medical cures and treatments than learning how to cook, the cabin presented a formidable challenge—a challenge Elizabeth now felt unwilling to meet. She was grateful to see her own surprise reflected in her husband's eyes.

Uncle Will cleared his throat and coughed, then Elizabeth realized he was waiting for her reaction. "This certainly is a snug little place," she observed. It would be impolite to bare her true feelings. Nevertheless, she longed to tell him exactly what she thought of the crude structure.

Jacob swatted angrily at a mosquito. "At least it will keep the bugs away," he said. "We'll start carrying up our belongings, Elizabeth."

The men left, and Elizabeth stood alone in the center of the single room, taking inventory. Aside from the built-in bed, nothing but a small table and solitary chair furnished the little log cabin.

She looked down at the puncheon floor. Dried pine needles and grit littered the rough-hewn wood. No broom stood in the corner, and Elizabeth certainly hadn't bothered to pack one among her belongings. She stepped outside and broke off a few pine branches to use in place of a corn broom. By the time Jacob and Uncle Will returned with a trunk, the floor was as free of dirt as was reasonably possible.

While the men went for the second trunk, Elizabeth found a linen tablecloth among her belongings and draped it over the table. It fell nearly to the floor all the way around, but made the cabin look lived-in. Bed linens came out next, and soon one entire side of the cabin appeared less stark. Pegs along another wall provided a place for hanging her bonnets and capes, but she decided not to bother unpacking any heavy wraps. She wondered why she had ever let Jacob talk her into coming to Riverton. By the time he and Uncle Will returned, she had determined to speak to Jacob as soon as possible about leaving on the next steamer.

Uncle Will wiped his shirt sleeve across his damp forehead. "I'll leave so you two can finish settling in. If you need anything, I'll be at the blockhouse." Pine needles crunched beneath his feet as he disappeared down the trail, leaving them in privacy. Elizabeth opened her mouth to tell Jacob that she wanted to go back to New York state, but closed it without a word when she saw him throw his jacket on the bed.

"Paper town," he said, disappointment flooding his face.

"Pardon?"

"Riverton is nothing but a paper town," he continued. "No tree-lined streets and frame houses. No parks and churches. No banks. It's nothing like that map Uncle Will sent us. All there is to the town is that dock, the blockhouse, and a handful of log cabins." Jacob plopped his valise on the bed and rummaged inside.

I knew it, Elizabeth muttered to herself. *We've been swindled*.

Jacob continued searching through his bag. Frustrated, he dumped the entire contents of the valise onto the bed. Pawing through the documents, he finally located a map and unrolled it on the table. He held it open as he pointed to a square in the center. "There it is, our lot." He tapped his finger on the

11

map. "The one I bought from Uncle Will, and it's right in the middle of a pine forest." He let go of the map and it rolled up by itself as he began pacing back and forth again. "Elizabeth, I wish you could have seen him, heard him. When Uncle Will and I got to the top of the bank with my trunk, we stopped to rest. He pointed off into the east, and said, 'Don't you see it, Jacob? The white clapboard houses and parks where the children play on swings and teeter-totters? Two churches, and the schoolhouse over on Center Avenue?' " Jacob moved his head from side to side. "The clapboard on all those houses is still growing in those white pines." Jacob walked to one of the walls, studied it a moment and gave it a whack with his fist. The force dislodged a clump of mud chink, which dropped to the floor with a thud.

Elizabeth swooped to retrieve it and tucked it into its hole between the logs. "I thought Cousin Agatha was exaggerating when she warned me about the wilderness. I never dreamed it meant this." She struggled to control her voice. "Jacob, you can't let Uncle Will do this to you, to *us!*" Her anger making her bold, she suddenly decided, "I'm going straight to the blockhouse and tell him he's got to give back the money you paid him for our lot. We can't live here!" She spun toward the door.

Jacob gripped her arm, turning her toward him. "No, Elizabeth. Let me do it," he insisted. "I got us into this predicament, I'll get us out. Just be patient. I know my Uncle Will, and if you go to him right now and demand our money back, you'll just make him angry. He'll say you haven't given Riverton a chance."

"And I don't intend to," she asserted. "I know he's your uncle, Jacob, but he really duped us." She searched the face of the man she loved, angry at her circumstances, but unable to blame him for their troubles. She let out a tired sigh. "But, I suppose you're right. You should be the one to tell him we aren't staying."

Jacob released her arm and took her hands in his. "Elizabeth, it will probably take a few days to book passage," he said, "and I'm going to wait until later to bring it up with Uncle Will." He squeezed her hands, and in a quiet tone, asked, "Can you stand it for just a little while?"

Her brows came together. "All right, for just a little while."

Resigned to life in the wilderness cabin for a few days, Elizabeth struggled to light a fire in the stick and mud fireplace, and wondered how women managed to prepare anything edible in such primitive conditions. Though Uncle Will had been charming when he had brought her live coals a few minutes before, she couldn't help resenting him. The "cozy honeymoon cabin" he had promised in his letter barely qualified as a dwelling. At least he had been thoughtful enough to stack kindling and firewood near the door before they arrived.

Jacob had gone with his uncle to borrow a wooden bucket and fetch water. Alone with her thoughts, Elizabeth tried to talk herself into thinking of her few days in Riverton as an adventure, rather than a trial. She continued fanning her coals, deep in thought, when someone knocked sharply on the door. She looked up to find Mrs. Langton standing in the open doorway. The woman held a covered iron pot with a thick potholder.

Mrs. Langton stepped inside, not waiting for Elizabeth's invitation. "I can tell just by looking at you, that you'll have to toughen up if you're going to survive the winter in this place," she clipped. Elizabeth started to get up. "Ah, ah! stay right there and tend those coals," Mrs. Langton ordered, carrying the pot to her and setting it on the hearth.

"But we're not—" Elizabeth started to tell Mrs. Langton she wouldn't be living in the wilderness come winter, when the woman cut her off.

"Here's a pot of chowder for your supper. You'll have to rewarm it once you get your fire kindled, but it'll relieve you from the burden of cooking on your first night here. Don't get the wrong idea, though. Come tomorrow, you'll have to do for yourself."

Mrs. Langton walked away so quickly, she had nearly reached the door when Elizabeth called after her, "Thank you, Mrs. Langton."

Without turning back, Mrs. Langton waved her thanks aside. She stepped out the door, then suddenly spun around and returned to face Elizabeth again. "By the way, if I were you, I'd go down to the riverbank before dusk settles in and pick some berries. They make a good dessert with chowder." She hurried out the door before Elizabeth could think to ask her where to look along the riverbank.

When Elizabeth's fire had finally kindled, she hung the pot of chowder on the crane and swung it over the flames, then searched through her trunk. Near the bottom, she located the old, large wooden bowl that Hattie, her father's cook and housekeeper, had insisted she would need. Without a moment's hesitation, she hurried toward the river. The clean pine essence cleared the musty odor from her head, and for the first time Elizabeth appreciated the abundance of white pines.

Unsure what variety of berries Mrs. Langton meant, Elizabeth searched through the undergrowth. Soon she recognized a thicket of wild blueberries and picked them as quickly as she could, stopping frequently to swat at the hordes of mosquitos that attacked her with a vengeance. The dual assault of the prickly bushes and mosquito bites soon took a toll on her hands, making them scratched and swollen. When she could no longer tolerate the pain, she scrambled to the top of the bank. She was disheartened at her small harvest, but at least she would have a dessert for Jacob tonight.

Elizabeth worried as she set her table with two green-painted china soup bowls and two silver spoons that she had retrieved from her trunk. This was the first meal she would serve Jacob as his new wife, and she wanted everything to look just right. Compared with the fancy hotel dining rooms they had eaten in recently, a bowl of chowder appeared entirely inadequate.

Jacob stepped inside the cabin and set a bucket of water on the floor. "There's a village well in the center of the clearing. I'll show you later." He inhaled deeply. "Mm, something smells great," he said, stepping beside Elizabeth as she ladled soup into each bowl.

"Mrs. Langton brought us some chowder," Elizabeth explained, replacing the cover on the pot of soup. She looked at the lone chair pulled up to the table. "Do we eat one at a time?"

"You sure can tell a bachelor lived here," Jacob said dryly, looking around. "For now, I'll use a trunk." He dragged one up to the table opposite Elizabeth, then held the chair for her. Once sitting across from her, he reached for her hands and held them tightly while he prayed. "Dear Heavenly Father, we thank you for bringing us safely to our destination, even if it isn't what we expected. Please be with us as we make new plans. Bless this food to our use, and bless Mrs. Langton for her thoughtfulness. In Jesus' name, Amen."

"Amen," Elizabeth added.

They had just taken their first sip of chowder when a loud knock sounded on the door. Simultaneously, they looked up to find the door opening and Uncle Will standing in the doorway.

Hesitantly, he stepped inside. "Sorry. Didn't realize you folks would be eating. I'll stop by later, or better yet, Jacob, you come down to the blockhouse to see me when you're done. We should talk."

"Yes, you should," Elizabeth blurted out before she could stop herself. Jacob gave her a warning look, and she pressed her lips into a fine line, resolving to keep better control of her tongue.

"We can talk now," Jacob suggested. "Elizabeth, can you please set a place for Uncle Will?"

Will looked at Elizabeth, then again at Jacob. "This is business, Jacob. Surely Elizabeth wouldn't be interested in what I have to say."

She bit her tongue to keep from contradicting him.

Jacob grinned at his uncle. "Elizabeth isn't like most young ladies today, Uncle Will. She's got a good head for business, and an interest in it, as well." Jacob turned to his wife. "Isn't that right, Elizabeth?" He pulled the second trunk up to the end of the table.

"If you don't mind, Uncle Will, I'd like to be included in the business talk," Elizabeth confirmed, pushing her anger at him aside. She knew she would accomplish far more with a pleasant attitude. "I've kept my father's accounts for years. He's a doctor and has done his share of real estate investing as well," she explained. "Since I was his only child, and my mother died when I was very young, Papa and I were very close. He used to explain his investments to me. As a result, I'm avidly interested in Jacob's business endeavors."

She searched her trunk for one more bowl, hoping that Uncle Will would stay so she could ask him why he thought Jacob's land in the middle of the forest was such a good investment. When he didn't budge from near the door, she added, "We're dining on Mrs. Langton's chowder tonight. It's very tasty."

Elizabeth's mention of chowder seemed to change Will's mind. "Guess I'll stay then," he decided, sitting on the trunk.

"Jacob," Will began, "I'm so glad you and Elizabeth came when you did. Why, your Riverton lot is just the start of your investment opportunities here."

"It is?" Jacob asked.

"Tell us more, Uncle Will," Elizabeth prodded, eager to know what could possibly make their Riverton land a worthwhile purchase.

He paused to sip his chowder, then continued. "The banking industry's just been turned on its ear, what with the New York banks suspending payment of silver and gold last month, and the other banks all falling right in line."

Jacob looked puzzled. "But if silver and gold are so scarce, where's the opportunity?"

"Under the general law here in Michigan," Will began, "banks can be chartered, and can issue banknotes without having to worry about silver and gold to back them." He looked at his nephew. "It's the perfect chance for us to open a bank together, Jacob."

Elizabeth voiced her suspicion. "It sounds like counterfeiting to me."

The corner of Will's mouth curved up. "There are some who look at it that way I suppose, but I prefer to see it as a legal, equitable way to finance improvements here in the interior of the state."

Jacob paused a moment before speaking. "How risky is it to start a new bank?"

Will leaned forward eagerly. "It's about as sure a thing as you can find. Expansion and development have to continue. There are over a thousand steamboat arrivals in Detroit each week, during the shipping season. Those thousands of people and tons of goods have to wind up *somewhere*. Why not here in the Saginaw Valley, at Riverton, where we can sell land, and make a fair profit? Jacob, you and I can start our own bank right here, along with some others, and provide a service to the residents of Riverton."

17

Elizabeth was disheartened to see Jacob's enthusiasm mounting. He began thoughtfully. "When my brother Henry received *his* endowment from Dad, he stayed in western New York and invested in real estate. But here in Michigan, you mean I can afford to own part of a bank?"

"You've got it, my boy. You'll even have enough left over to buy part of Riverton from me, if you want. I'll sell the land to you at two dollars and fifty cents per acre. That's a sound deal. I understand some developers are already up to ten dollars per acre or more."

Elizabeth spoke up. "Slow down, you two. You're moving far too fast for me. Uncle Will," she fastened her eyes on his, "we're not interested in—"

Jacob cut her off. "We'll have to think it over, Uncle Will, and let you know what we've decided." He tapped the leg of her chair with the toe of his boot, his signal that she should save her opinions for their private discussion.

"You do that. I'll talk to you later. Thanks for the supper, Elizabeth." Will rose from the table.

"You're welcome, Uncle Will."

Elizabeth and Jacob saw him out the door, then Jacob turned to her. "Just think, Elizabeth, we could own half of Riverton, if we want." He took her hands in his. "There could be a town out there with a street named after you, and a school—"

"A town?" She pulled her hands from his. "Jacob, we'll be old and gray before Riverton amounts to a whole town."

"It won't take as long as you think, Elizabeth. You heard Uncle Will. People are coming to Michigan by the thousands. Before you know it, Riverton will be a bustling little community."

Elizabeth moved to the table and began clearing the dishes. "I have no intention of living here in the wilderness long enough to see Riverton become a bustling community. The sooner you get us on a steamer out of here, the happier I'll be." She clanked the bowls together. Jacob leaned over the table. She could feel his eyes boring into her as she worked, but she refused to look up.

"Fine. I'll tell Uncle Will you don't want any part of his town," Jacob said tersely, "but I think we'd be turning our backs on a good opportunity." His heels clicked against the pine boards as he walked to the door. "I'm going for a walk to think it all over."

Elizabeth looked up, watching him disappear down the path, and thought she would never be happy again until they had left Michigan.

CHAPTER 2

JACOB WALKED ALONE along the riverbank. His uncle's blockhouse lay several yards behind him. He had purposely avoided going there, knowing he needed time alone to think. Never before had he walked out on Elizabeth in anger. He loved her so much, that he missed being with her the very moment he had left the cabin, but he couldn't go back to her until he had sorted out his problems.

For nearly a year, he and Elizabeth had planned to move to the Saginaw Valley. Uncle Will had sent him frequent letters detailing his plans for Riverton, encouraging him to bring his bride, promising him opportunities he could never match back East. For months, he had looked forward to being a part of Riverton, and now that the prospects looked better, he wanted to stay. Sure, Jacob had been disappointed to find that Riverton wasn't quite what Uncle Will had described, but once he had heard Uncle Will talk about starting a bank and selling him land, he didn't mind that the village wasn't as built-up as he had expected. If he didn't grasp the chance to make money on Riverton's growth, someone else surely would.

Besides, he wanted to prove himself to his older brother. He and Henry had always competed against one another. Henry had done well for himself in real estate investments in New York, and had criticized Jacob's judgment when he bought land in Michigan. Jacob was determined to make a success of his venture West, determined to show Henry he had been wrong.

Jacob's biggest concern, however, was for Elizabeth. He wanted only the best for her, and as he saw it, the best way to get it was to stay in the Saginaw Valley and invest in a growing community. He wondered if Elizabeth could ever learn to like Riverton. There seemed to be no answer that would please them both. Though it was Jacob's responsibility as head of the household to make the final decision, he wanted his wife to have a say in their future. Unfortunately, on this issue, they seemed to be in total disagreement.

Unable to come to any definite conclusions, Jacob knelt in the grass on the riverbank and talked to God. "Dear Heavenly Father, please be with Elizabeth and me as we make decisions for our future. Please show us what we should do, and guide us always. In Jesus' name, Amen."

Jacob got to his feet and wandered toward the blockhouse. Dusk had started to fall, and lanterns shone from the windows. He could hear his uncle stacking barrels of supplies Captain Winthrop had offloaded that afternoon, and decided to go inside and offer his help. When they had moved the last of the barrels from the dock into the blockhouse, Will looked at his nephew with an inquiring eye.

"Jacob, what's the matter? You've been awful quiet." Will leaned against a barrel and folded his arms across his chest.

Jacob moved his head slowly from side to side. "Nothing you can help me with, Uncle Will." He stared down at the toe of his boot, usually polished to a shine, now dusty like his Uncle Will's.

"How's Elizabeth doing? Has she threatened yet to take the first boat out?"

Jacob looked up surprised. "How did you know?"

Uncle Will shrugged. "All the women want to go home at first. Can't say I blame them. This is a rough place, especially come winter."

"Elizabeth wants me to book passage for New York as soon as possible," Jacob commented, clearly dismayed. "I told her it would take a few days, and she's resigned herself to that, but she's anxious to leave."

"What about you?"

Jacob hesitated before answering. "I don't feel quite the same as she does."

"Meaning you want to stay, and she doesn't," Will concluded.

"I guess that pretty well sums it up."

"It isn't going to be easy, or cheap, getting from here back to Stockport," Will warned his nephew. "You could wait for days in Detroit for passage to Buffalo, but I've got good connections with one of the captains that runs that route and I can have him reserve two berths for you. You'll have to be patient, though, this time of year. It's much cheaper and easier to get space later in the season. If you could talk Elizabeth into staying until fall, you'll save a substantial amount of money."

Jacob's brows moved together. "How soon do you think we could leave?"

Will's head moved slowly from side to side. "Hard to say. Could take as long as a month . . . by then maybe Elizabeth will decide to stay," Will conjectured.

"Hmph. I doubt it."

"Stranger things have happened, Jacob. Just take it a day at a time, and try to be extra considerate of Elizabeth. Encourage her to get to know the people here—especially Mrs. Clarke, the reverend's wife—she's a real kind lady. The settlers of Riverton are good people, always helping one another. I think Elizabeth will like them, if she just gives them a chance, and I know they'll like her. After a few weeks, this could seem like home to her."

"Not likely, Uncle Will. I appreciate your advice, but I'm not going to get my hopes up. Elizabeth is a very headstrong young lady."

"You do the best you can to help her adjust, Jacob, and I'll see what I can do about your passage home, in case she doesn't want to stay after all." He patted his nephew's shoulder. "As long as you're here, you could help me clear some land. We might as well get to work on your lot. Why don't you come down in the morning when you're ready to start work."

Jacob nodded. "See you tomorrow, Uncle Will."

As he worked his way up the path toward the cabin, he wondered how Elizabeth would react when he told her it could be as long as a month before they would be able to leave for New York. He wanted desperately to avoid upsetting her further. As he walked and thought, a plan formulated in his mind that he believed would appeal to his wife's conservative nature, while convincing her to accept Riverton as her home for several more weeks.

After Jacob had walked out the door, Elizabeth washed the supper dishes and cleaned up Mrs. Langton's pot. Her anger over their disappointments at Riverton had subsided during the time she had spent alone, and she regretted now that she allowed her emotions to take over, rather than discussing their circumstances calmly with Jacob. It wasn't his fault that Riverton was such a wilderness, that their cabin

23

was so crude, that Uncle Will had deceived them. It was Jacob's uncle who had angered her, not Jacob. She was wishing that her husband would come back so she could tell him that when he walked through the door.

"Jacob—"

"Elizabeth—"

They both spoke at once.

Jacob came to her, placing his hands on her shoulders. "I'm sorry I walked out on you."

"I'm sorry I was upset with you when it was your uncle who made me angry," Elizabeth admitted.

Jacob laid his hand alongside her face. "Elizabeth, I love you so much, I can't bear to see you upset." He pulled her close, and she rested her cheek on his solid chest, comforted by the rhythm of his heart. He kissed the top of her head, then leaned away. "Let's sit on the bed. I want to talk to you about our trip back to Stockport. Uncle Will had a good suggestion for us."

She gave him a puzzled look. "I thought you were going to wait to bring that up with your uncle."

He ushered her to the bed and sat down, then pulled her down beside him. With his arm around her waist, he began to explain. "I didn't bring it up with him at all. Elizabeth, Uncle Will knows it's hard for women to adjust to life here, that's how he guessed you wanted to go back to New York without my having to tell him. But it's going to take time and money to book passage to Buffalo."

"I was afraid of that," Elizabeth commented, rising to pace across the floor. She turned to face her husband. "How long will it take to get reservations?"

Jacob moved to her. "Well, that depends."

"Depends on what?"

Jacob brushed a dark brown tress from her face. "I'm thinking that you're a very frugal woman. Remember how you kept warning me not to spend so much money when we were traveling here?"

Elizabeth nodded.

"I figured you'd be interested in going back to New York when it's cheapest."

Elizabeth sighed. "I'm almost afraid to ask when that is."

Jacob pulled her into the circle of his arms. "I know you're anxious to get back, but we'd have to spend the next month here anyway, so we might as well wait until the rates drop in the fall."

Elizabeth moaned. A month! Until fall? She wanted to cry out in frustration, but responded as calmly as she could to the news. "It's hard to imagine staying here . . . that long," she nearly choked on her own words, "but you do have a point."

Jacob pulled her closer. "And I have another point, too." His voice grew quiet.

Elizabeth tried to forget the bad news and wrapped her arms about his neck. "What's that, Jacob?"

Without warning, he whisked her off her feet and held her in his arms. "It's time for bed."

Elizabeth relaxed in the cradle of Jacob's strong arms, thankful that in the difficult days to come, they would have their love for each other to see them through.

Early the next morning, Elizabeth arose to prepare breakfast while Jacob slept. Corn cakes seemed the easiest choice. She rekindled her fire and measured the corn meal and salt from the limited supply of staples they had brought with them from Detroit, then set a pot of water over the fire to boil. Though she tried to work quietly, it seemed like every pan she touched rattled or banged, and soon Jacob was up and dressing.

"I'm sorry I woke you, Jacob. I didn't mean to."

Jacob tucked his checkered shirt into his denim trousers, then moved to Elizabeth's side and drew her close. "No need to be sorry. It's time I got up

25

anyway." He planted a good-morning kiss on her upturned face and squeezed her shoulders. "I'm going to fetch water and wash up." Glancing at the table strewn with cooking utensils, he added, "I'll stay outside, though. I'd hate to get in the way of a cook at work."

Elizabeth was thankful to have the cabin to herself while she finished preparing breakfast, because cooking made her nervous. She had almost no experience at it. Her mother had died when she was small, and her father's housekeeper, Hattie, had seen to the cooking ever since. She was glad that Jacob wasn't watching her awkward efforts as she spilled hot water on the floor and slopped corn batter on the tablecloth. Finally, she set the frying pan on the coals to heat and dropped a chunk of lard into it to melt.

A few minutes later, she spooned the corn batter into the pan in lumps. While she was waiting for the corn cakes to finish cooking on the first side, she discovered the blueberries she had picked last night. She had forgotten to serve them for supper, so decided to wash them and serve them for breakfast. She turned the corn cakes over, then stepped outside to see if Jacob had returned with the bucket of water, but he was not there. Carrying the large wooden bowl with her, she ventured a few steps down the lane in front of their cabin, wondering whether the village well would soon come into sight. A few moments later, she saw that the path ended at another settler's cabin door.

She turned back, remembering it was time to check on the frying pan. The air was tainted with a burnt smell as she walked in the door. Setting the bowl of blueberries on the table, she grabbed a towel and pulled the pan away from the fire. With spatula in hand, she lifted a corn cake to look at its bottom side. Black! Elizabeth's heart plummeted.

Just then, Jacob returned. He sniffed the air and

casually commented, "Hmm, smells interesting. What are we having for breakfast?"

Elizabeth set the frying pan on the hearth, placed a cover over it, and stepped beside the table. Lifting the bowl for him to see, she answered, "Blueberries. Did you fetch the water? I'd like to wash them before we eat."

Jacob eyed the blueberries, then the frying pan on the hearth before answering. "It's right outside the door. I'll get it for you."

Elizabeth prayed Jacob would not look inside the frying pan, she was so embarrassed by her futile efforts at cooking breakfast. He seemed to sense her plight. Setting the water bucket inside the door, he sat quietly on the bed organizing the documents in his valise until she called him to the table.

When they sat across from one another holding hands for grace, Jacob's prayer was simple, "Dear Heavenly Father, we thank You for Your blueberries, and in days to come, look forward to Your increased blessings. In Jesus' name, Amen." Jacob tasted a spoonful of the fruit and nodded approval. "Sweet and juicy. Wonderful, Elizabeth."

Elizabeth didn't know whether to laugh or cry. "Oh, Jacob, you needn't pretend with me. I'm a failure as a cook. A complete failure!" She went to the hearth and picked up the frying pan, intending to show him her burnt disaster.

"Put that down, Elizabeth, and come back to the table." Jacob spoke with a level tone. She gave him a baffled look, then did as he said. He reached for her hand, then quietly asked her, "Elizabeth, how many times have you cooked a meal?"

"Well . . . none. Jacob, what are you getting at? You know I never cooked in Stockport—that Hattie did everything."

"Of course I knew. That's exactly the point. I don't care if your first breakfast didn't turn out quite the

27

way you wanted. After a while, you'll be good at it. I bet you'll even learn to make coffee."

"Coffee!" Elizabeth shrieked. "I forgot to make your coffee." She jumped up from the table and rummaged through her supplies until she found the ground coffee they had bought in Detroit. When she looked up, Jacob had already located the coffee pot and filled it with water. Together, they measured out the grounds, then Jacob set the pot over the fire. Soon after, they chatted over freshly brewed mugs of coffee.

Jacob suggested, "Let's look up Mrs. Clarke after breakfast. Uncle Will says you'd like her."

"I need to look up Mrs. Langton, too, so I can return her soup kettle."

"Good point. While you're getting to know some of the ladies in the settlement, Uncle Will and I are going to start clearing the land I bought from him. If we don't stay in Michigan, I'll have to sell the property, and improved land will be worth a lot more."

A distraught look registered on Elizabeth's face. "Jacob, you said, *'if* we don't stay in Michigan.' We're going back to New York come fall, at least that's what you told me last night."

Jacob's face reddened. "I . . . I . . . you know what I meant." He got up from the table. "I'm going to find out where the Langtons and Clarkes live while you clean up. I'll be back for you in a few minutes."

Elizabeth dumped the burnt corn cakes into the fire then set the pan to soaking with hot water and soap. While she washed the breakfast dishes, she couldn't help but wonder whether Jacob still had hopes of staying in Michigan.

After they had first arrived, he had said they would stay only a few days, then last night, it had stretched to several weeks. Now he sounded as if they might not leave at all. There was nothing to be gained by making an issue over it now. She was resigned to living in Riverton until fall. As time went by, and the departure date grew nearer, she would plan for their return to Stockport. For now, all she could think about was learning to survive from one meal to the next, one day to the next, in this tiny wilderness community.

Jacob returned for Elizabeth and took her to Mrs. Langton's cabin, where she returned the pot with a new potholder tucked under the cover. Mrs. Langton thanked her for returning her kettle, and seemed pleased with the new hot pad, but barely wasted a moment away from pounding her corn on congenialities.

At Mrs. Clarke's cabin, the latch string hung outside the door, an invitation for callers to let themselves in, but Jacob and Elizabeth felt it best to knock, instead.

Mrs. Clarke greeted them with a friendly smile. "Jacob, Elizabeth, come in, come in."

Jacob explained, "I'm on my way to work with my uncle, Mrs. Clarke, thank you anyway. Elizabeth would like to visit with you for awhile, though."

"Then, please do come again, Jacob. My husband is with the chief of the Chippewa village this morning. Perhaps you can return when he is here as well."

"Thank you. I'd enjoy that."

Elizabeth said goodbye to Jacob, then stepped inside her neighbor's cabin.

Mrs. Clarke motioned her to a chair at the table. As she took down a cup and saucer for Elizabeth and filled it from a pot kept warm off to one side of her fire, she spoke in friendly tones. "Will Morgan told us you and Jacob were newly married. How I remember the joys, and the challenges of being a new wife especially the trouble I had learning to cook. The first dinner I made was a disaster!" Infectious laughter bubbled in her throat, and soon Elizabeth was chuckling with the jolly lady.

"Until last night, Jacob and I have been eating on boats, and in hotel dining rooms. Soon after we arrived here, Mrs. Langton brought us a pot of chowder, so I didn't have a disastrous first dinner, but when I tried to make breakfast this morning . . ." She shook her head. "My corn cakes weren't fit for a dog, I'm afraid." Elizabeth took a sip of tea, then asked, "Do you know Mrs. Langton very well?"

"The Langtons have lived here almost as long as we have, nearly two years. Why do you ask?"

"Mrs. Langton seems to have such a brusque manner, and I couldn't help but notice that she gave Jacob and me a good looking-over when we first arrived. Quite frankly, I was surprised she brought us the soup." Elizabeth smiled. "She didn't waste a minute delivering it to our cabin. She was gone almost before I could thank her. Still, I got an uneasy feeling when we returned her kettle this morning."

Mrs. Clarke waved Elizabeth's concern aside. "Clara Langton must approve of you if she brought you chowder last night. Don't let her quick manner put you off, she's a very considerate lady, always helping others. She's a hard worker, too, organizing cabin-raisings, barn-raisings, corn-huskings in the fall and sugar-bush parties in the spring. We have such fun at our get-togethers. You'll see."

Elizabeth didn't tell her that she wouldn't be there long enough to find out.

Mrs. Clarke continued, "Once Clara Langton gets to know you a little better, she'll warm to you and open up some."

Elizabeth was thoughtful.

"What is it dear? Is there something on your mind?"

"Mrs. Clarke, do you think . . ." Elizabeth hesitated. "Could you teach me how to cook?"

"I'd be glad to teach you, my dear. What would you like to—"

30

Without warning, a young Indian woman burst through the door clutching a tiny bundle. Elizabeth's heart lurched, seeing a Chippewa for the first time. The Indian woman spoke emotionally in her native tongue to Mrs. Clarke, then showed her the contents of her bundle.

Mrs. Clarke paled when she saw what the woman had brought her. "Her baby is dead. From smallpox!" she exclaimed.

CHAPTER 3

ELIZABETH SPOKE URGENTLY. "My father is a physician back East. He supplied me with some of the smallpox vaccine. How many people live at her village?"

"About a hundred, but some of the men are off hunting and fishing. Only seventy-five or eighty would be there right now. Why?"

"If smallpox is really what her child died from, everyone living in this area should receive a vaccination. I've got enough for our village, and theirs, too. Ask her if I can see her baby, to be sure it was smallpox."

Mrs. Clarke interpreted Elizabeth's request to see the dead infant to the Indian mother.

"No!" The Indian woman responded emphatically in English, clutching the lifeless form.

"Can she understand English, then?" Elizabeth asked.

"Beloved-of-the-Forest is just learning our language, and only understands a few words," Mrs. Clarke explained. "I can assure you, the pock marks on her baby are from smallpox."

"Can you explain that her people will be spared the spotted fever, if they'll submit to the vaccination?"

Mrs. Clarke translated, then interpreted the Indian's answer. "She says only her father, the Chief, can decide whether the village should receive the white man's prevention for spotted fever. I'll go with her now and my husband and I will explain it to her father. If he agrees, I will come back for you. Is it difficult to administer?"

"It is easily given. The virus is introduced into a bleeding scratch on the arm. Within a few seconds the patient is immunized. Have you received the vaccination yet, Mrs. Clarke?"

"No, I haven't."

"Wait here a moment while I fetch the vaccine from my trunk."

A few minutes later, Mrs. Clarke rolled up her sleeve for Elizabeth to vaccinate her, then left with Beloved-of-the-Forest.

While Elizabeth waited for Mrs. Clarke to return from the Indian village, she looked for Jacob and Uncle Will, thinking she could immunize the other residents of Riverton before Mrs. Clarke returned. She and Jacob had been immunized by her father before the trip, and now Elizabeth whispered a prayer of thanks for the assurance that they need not worry about contracting the dreaded smallpox, and a prayer of help that the others would be immunized in time.

Elizabeth went to the blockhouse where Uncle Will had said yesterday that he could be found, but no one was there. She proceeded farther south along the river bank. The sound of ax blades cutting rhythmically through standing timber drew her attention.

She worked her way through the trees until she could see Uncle Will, and picked out Jacob's shirt and trousers through the pine boughs. As she went toward her husband she thought how he was beginning to look like a backwoodsman himself.

Uncle Will saw her first and called to Jacob. They leaned their axes against a tree and joined her. Elizabeth spoke solemnly as she explained, "There's an outbreak of smallpox among the Chippewas."

"Oh, no," Jacob moaned.

She looked at Uncle Will. "My father sent enough supplies for me to vaccinate the settlers at Riverton, and the Chippewas, too, if they'll agree. Reverend and Mrs. Clarke are asking the chief's permission now. Perhaps I could vaccinate the Riverton residents while I wait for word."

"Come with me to the blockhouse," Uncle Will suggested. "I'll ring the bell there. It will be the easiest way to gather everyone at once."

A short while later, the other Riverton residents gathered near the blockhouse, abuzz with speculation.

A bushy bearded, gruff-looking man slipped a bottle from his pocket and took a nip, then wiped the back of his hand across his matted mustache and stepped forward, coming face to face with Will.

"This'd better be import'nt, Morgan," the man slurred. "I got better things t'do 'n come running 'cause you rung the bell." A meek and timid woman, whom Elizabeth assumed was his wife, shrank back, her eyes downcast. A toddling son clung to her skirt.

A hush fell over the gathering as Will addressed the fellow boldly. "It's important, Tyler. Unless you want a case of the smallpox."

The women gasped in horror and whispered among themselves.

Captain Langton spoke up. "Who's got the pox?"

Elizabeth stepped forward to answer. "Beloved-of-the-Forest's baby died of smallpox this morning."

Will spoke again. "You're just doggone lucky my nephew and his new wife arrived here when they did. Elizabeth's father is a doctor back East. He gave her enough supplies to vaccinate us all."

Tyler retorted, "I ain't never been to no doctor of

med-cin, and I shore won't let no female imitator touch me, neither!'' The half-drunk man turned to leave.

Will shouted after him, ''You're a fool, Tyler!''

''What's 'at?'' Tyler swung around, fists balled.

''I said you're nothing but a drunk, lazy fool.'' Tyler swung wildly at him. Will ducked. Two other men ran to Tyler and twisted his arms behind him. Will shouted at the restrained man. ''I *know* you went to the Chippewa camp to trade firewater for that new dog of yours. You've exposed your family. At least let your wife and son take the vaccination.'' Will took Tyler's bottle from his pocket and threatened to pour its contents onto the ground. ''What'll it be, Tyler?''

Tyler strained against his captors. They slammed him onto the ground where he lay pinned on his back. ''All right. The wife 'n boy. But keep that imposter away from me.''

There was no further resistance. The other settlers received their vaccinations gratefully and dispersed. Mrs. Tyler waited with her son until last. By then, her husband had wandered off to indulge again in his bottle.

When Mrs. Tyler stepped forward with her young son, Elizabeth noticed the worn, patched, but clean clothing they wore. Bruises showed on her arm after she pulled up her sleeve. A knowing look passed between them, and without asking, Elizabeth was certain that Mrs. Tyler had been victimized during her husband's drunken rages.

The woman spoke quietly as she rolled her sleeve down. ''I'm mighty thankful to you for this.'' She pushed a loose strand of straight, brown hair back toward her tangled bun. ''I apologize for what my husband said about you.''

Elizabeth accepted the apology with a nod. ''If there's any way I can help you, call on me, won't you?'' Mrs. Tyler averted her eyes, and Elizabeth read the signs almost instinctively. Asking for help would only infuriate Mr. Tyler, and his wife and son would suffer for it. Elizabeth felt helpless as the mother started across the clearing, head down, small son clinging to her side.

Mrs. Clarke returned for Elizabeth, finding her and Jacob at the blockhouse. "The Chief has accepted the vaccination," she explained eagerly.

"Good. Will you take us to their village now?"

Mrs. Clarke led Elizabeth and Jacob along the narrow Indian trail on the riverbank that would take them to the Chippewa settlement. As they walked, Mrs. Clarke explained how she and her husband, Ben, had been working with the Indians for the past two years, teaching them English, showing them how to cultivate crops, and sharing the gospel with them. "So far the Indians haven't accepted Christ, but we're not going to give up," she said.

Several minutes later, they entered the Chippewa village, dotted with dome-shaped huts. As they passed one of the birch bark wigwams, several dogs lying in the dirt behind the hut growled at them.

Elizabeth moved closer to Jacob. "They surely don't look like family pets. They look like wolves, almost."

Mrs. Clarke explained, "They're a crossbreed. Brother-of-the-Wolf raises nearly all the dogs in this village. Indians don't make pets of their dogs like we do. They're considered a source of food, or a means of pulling a sledge in winter."

Mrs. Clarke led Elizabeth to a long building at the center of the village. "Ben is in the council lodge talking with the Chief. They're expecting us." She lifted the heavy fur skin that hung over the opening at the narrow end. Inside, shafts of light streamed from the smoke holes above, and at the far end, Elizabeth could just make out the dim figures of the Reverend Clarke and the Chief. She waited for Mrs. Clarke to lead the way.

Mr. Clarke spoke to the Chief in his own language, while his wife translated for Elizabeth and Jacob.

"Great Chief, our friend, Elizabeth, has come to help make your people safe from the smallpox that has already brought one death to your village."

The Chief spoke to Elizabeth in solemn tones, pausing occasionally for Mr. Clarke's translation. "Our medicine man is powerless against the spotted fever. My people thank you for offering your help. Soon, they will gather here."

As if by magic, word spread among the villagers to come to the council house. Elizabeth noted how the women greased and carefully plaited their ebony hair. The men were robust and broad featured. Many of them were over six feet tall.

Of all the braves, one in particular stood out. Mrs. Clarke identified him as Brother-of-the-Wolf, the same one who raised the dogs. His sleek, muscular physique spoke of the hours he had trained as a hunter.

The last Chippewa Elizabeth vaccinated was Beloved-of-the-Forest. When she finished, the Indian woman hesitated before she left, and spoke to Elizabeth through Mrs. Clarke.

"Thank you, daughter of white medicine man. Though it is too late for my child, the kindness you have shown today will save many of my people." She bowed her head and left on quiet moccasins.

After Beloved-of-the-Forest had gone from the lodge, Elizabeth spoke to Mrs. Clarke. "She seems to have changed her attitude about me since this morning, when she wouldn't even let me look at her baby."

Mrs. Clarke nodded. "When I came with her to her father, he impressed upon her how generous your offer was, and how important the vaccinations were. He told her how, in times past, whole tribes had been wiped out by smallpox, and that their village could be destroyed in a few days if it weren't for your help."

"I'm grateful he understood the importance of the vaccine," Elizabeth said.

Having vaccinated nearly a hundred Indians, Elizabeth, Jacob, and Mrs. Clarke returned to Riverton. When Elizabeth prepared for bed later that evening, she was thoughtful.

"I'm thankful we're among these peaceful Chippewas, Jacob. Even their language is musical. When they speak, it's almost in song."

"Uncle Will says they're remarkable hunters and fishermen," Jacob added. "He says for a Spanish quarter, you can buy a fish from them large enough to feed a family of nine!"

"It's no wonder those braves are strong. They'd give even the toughest New York farm boys a struggle in arm wrestling," Elizabeth laughed. "One brave, Brother-of-the-Wolf, appears to be phenomenally strong. I've never seen such muscles."

"Speaking of muscles," Jacob said as he bolted the cabin door, "I can feel the lameness in mine from swinging an ax today." He moved his shoulders in a circular motion and winced. "Do you have any liniment in your medical supplies that might help?"

"Father wouldn't have let me leave without it. I'll rub it on for you."

Jacob removed his shirt and lay face down on the bed. "Ah, just what I needed," he murmured, as Elizabeth massaged the balm into his sore muscles. She continued massaging him until his even breathing told her he had fallen asleep.

Elizabeth returned the medicine to her trunk, then crawled onto the bed beside Jacob. She lay awake for a while, thinking how different their lives in the Saginaw River settlement were from the lives they had left in Stockport.

The plaintive howl of wolves nearby, and the nearly human scream of a panther provided the lullaby to which Elizabeth drifted asleep.

38

In what seemed only moments later, raucous yells and fierce pounding on the bolted door jarred Elizabeth and Jacob awake. Jacob scrambled out of bed. Elizabeth began to follow. "Stay put, Elizabeth!" he ordered. She perched on the edge of the bed, trembling with fright, and straining to see in the light of the low-burning fire.

Jacob maneuvered the two trunks and the chair in front of the door. He armed himself with a piece of firewood and positioned himself between the small table and the bed. Loud assaults on the door continued.

Elizabeth stared, wide-eyed with fright, as the door ripped from its hinges and split crosswise in half. "Brother-of-the-Wolf!" she cried, panicking at his glassy-eyed fury. The Indian sprawled over the trunks, then quickly righted himself in a semi-crouched position brandishing the gleaming blade of a hunting knife.

"He's drunk," Jacob shouted, dodging the brave's uncoordinated lunges, keeping the table between them. Brother-of-the-Wolf lunged again at Jacob, knocking the firewood club from his hand. Elizabeth screamed as Jacob ducked the stabbing blade, then upended the table between himself and his attacker.

Using the tabletop as a shield, Jacob avoided Brother-of-the-Wolf's stabbing blade. The Indian's knife tip embedded itself in the table. Enraged, Brother-of-the-Wolf wrenched the table from Jacob and sent it crashing against the cabin wall. Jacob scrambled across the floor, avoiding the brave's wide-swinging fist, and grabbed the small chair, holding it in front of him.

Elizabeth scrambled for her iron frying pan. Brother-of-the-Wolf hurled the chair away, throwing Jacob against the cabin wall. Seeing Jacob's motionless form, Elizabeth screamed.

Brother-of-the-Wolf yanked open the top of one

trunk. Crazed, he flung its contents by the fistful across the room. Elizabeth's lacy nightgown landed in a heap on the hearth ashes. Her bone china soup bowls crashed one at a time against the cabin walls. Angry grunts accompanied Brother-of-the-Wolf's assault on the second trunk containing the medical supplies. His back was to her now. All his attention centered on the trunk latches, which frustrated him in his rage. Jacob moaned and started to move.

Elizabeth crept behind the Indian, and as he flung the trunk lid open, she swung her iron frying pan against his back. He turned in a rage and Jacob, who was on his knees, spotted the firewood club and, in one swift motion, grabbed it and crashed it down on the Indian's head.

Elizabeth dropped the frying pan and collapsed on the bed in shock. Her skin grew clammy and her stomach felt nauseated. Jacob sat beside her, holding her against his chest, stroking her tousled hair.

"It's all over, sweetheart. Everything's all right."

Elizabeth trembled in his arms. "What did he want?"

"Alcohol. Uncle Will warned me today about the Indians when they get into the drink. 'Makes them more cussed than a Michigan black bear,' Uncle Will says. I laughed when he said it, but now I know he's right."

"But Jacob, why *us*?"

"You vaccinated Brother-of-the-Wolf today, didn't you?"

"Yes, but . . . ?"

"He knew you had medical supplies. I bet he thought you had whiskey among them."

Elizabeth's eyes widened, then gales of nervous laughter overtook her as she released the tension that had built up inside her. Brother-of-the-Wolf stirred, moaning.

"He learned a very hard lesson tonight about my

medical supplies. Alcohol, common prescription that it might be, is not one of my approved remedies."

Elizabeth helped Jacob drag the beleaguered brave outside their cabin door. They hung a drape across the door, then crawled back into bed, to lie in the comfort of each other's arms.

Several days after Jacob had first seen the land he had bought from his uncle, he stood back and looked at the lot with pride. He and Uncle Will had finished clearing a building site in the center of the plot. If only Elizabeth would agree to stay permanently, he could start building a house there, and a pretty setting it would be too, surrounded by tall white pines and banked by the river on one side. Few settlers in the Saginaw Valley owned such a scenic plot of land, he certain.

Uncle Will, who had been down to the river to refresh himself after a hard day's toil, ambled back to the lot, then rested his boot on a stump near Jacob. "Tomorrow we can start digging the foundation for your new house, Jacob."

Jacob gave his uncle a puzzled look.

"Now that you've gone to the trouble of clearing a site, you might as well make the most of it. You'll get a lot more for your land when you sell it, if you've put something on it that's worthwhile, and I don't mean one of those twelve by twenty-four foot cabins, either. I mean a real frame house."

Jacob moved his head from side to side and grinned. "You really are a joker, aren't you, Uncle Will. You know Elizabeth hasn't agreed to stay beyond fall. Just think how upset she'd be if she found out I was investing our savings into a house here in Riverton."

"Who's to say she's going to find out? You could just not tell her, at least not for a while. By the time fall rolls around, she'll be all adjusted to our little community."

Jacob's brows moved together. "You know there's no guarantee of that, Uncle Will. As much as I'd like to stay in Riverton, I've got to take her wishes into consideration, and I can't assume she'll ever be happy enough here to make this her permanent home."

"Well, Jacob, you can't wait forever for her to decide. If you wait until fall to find out if she's going to be happy here, it will be too late to build. You'd better start now. You can always sell it for a lot more than it costs you. The way prices are going, a new house in these parts is one of the best investments a man can make."

"I'll give it some thought, Uncle Will."

"Why don't we start on the foundation tomorrow, then. That much won't cost you anything but a lame back. Once that's done, you can decide if you want to go ahead with the rest of the house. And," he added quickly, "there's no need to worry Elizabeth about it seeing as how she might not understand the logic of it—and it won't be costing anything."

"But she's bound to find out if she comes wandering over here to see me for one reason or another, although after the scare we had the other night she's stayed pretty close to home."

Uncle Will grinned mischievously. "You're right, it's pretty dangerous around here, what with falling trees, and Indians—and there are even bears in these woods. I think I'd tell her not to come near your new lot, because she might get hurt. If she needs you, tell her she should ring the bell at the blockhouse and you'll come running. Now get on home and eat a good supper. I'll see you in the morning."

As Jacob walked to the cabin, he felt guilty that he would even consider starting to build a house without consulting Elizabeth, but Uncle Will did have a good point. He *could* get a better price for his land with something decent on it, should he sell.

He would have to emphasize to Elizabeth that she

should not come to the lot. She hadn't been by since the day they had learned about the smallpox at the Indian village, but he should have told her from the start to use the blockhouse bell for her own safety. He would now. And no matter how guilty it made him feel, it was in their best interests if he just left off the fact that they were no longer chopping down pines, but had begun digging dirt.

A few days later, Elizabeth awoke feeling nauseated. Each of the next several mornings the feeling returned, and she suspected she might be pregnant. She decided not to say anything to Jacob until she was sure.

Elizabeth spent many hours with Mrs. Clarke during the first several days at Riverton learning the art of pioneer survival. Mrs. Clarke gave of her time unselfishly, teaching Elizabeth how to prepare meals using the natural foods abundant in the area, such as young basswood leaves, aromatic sassafras, and the foliage of mustard for a mess of greens. A milk cow, shared with another family, provided her with fresh dairy products. These with some salt pork and sap vinegar as a condiment nourished Elizabeth and Jacob, and frequently Uncle Will too, at many dinners.

In return for the meals she had prepared for Uncle Will, he had built and hung shelves for her, and had made her three new chairs. Though he seemed eager to make her stay in Riverton more comfortable, Elizabeth suspected there could be an ulterior motive behind his gestures, something more than assuring himself a continued place at their table.

When Elizabeth decided her pregnancy was progressing normally, she knew she must soon tell Jacob about it. But first, she decided to seek advice from Mrs. Clarke in preparing baby clothing for the new arrival. It would be a good way to fill her time in the remaining weeks until their return to Stockport. Then she would set the pieces out where Jacob would be sure to notice and surprise him. One morning, she paid Mrs. Clarke a visit.

"Tea, Elizabeth?" Mrs. Clarke always offered some, freshly steeped.

"I'd love some, thank you." She sipped from the dainty china cup Mrs. Clarke had somehow managed to bring safely all the way from Albany.

"Mrs. Clarke." Elizabeth started slowly. "I need some advice. I need to make some baby clothes."

Mrs. Clarke broke into a grin and covered Elizabeth's hand with her pudgy one. "Elizabeth, that's wonderful news. How long have you known?"

"Several days," Elizabeth beamed. Somehow, sharing the news with Mrs. Clarke made her pregnancy more real. "I haven't told Jacob yet," she half whispered, putting her finger to her lips. "I thought it best to wait a while. But I'm feeling fine, and I thought if I could get a baby kimono and some diapers ready, I could set them out, and let him take the hint."

"What can I help you with? Cutting the pattern? Sewing the seams? Whichever part you like least, I'll do. Sewing has always come naturally to me."

"I'm reluctant to admit I don't sew very well. I suppose I might have learned if my mother hadn't died when I was five."

Mrs. Clarke nodded. "Did your papa raise you alone, then?"

Elizabeth shook her head. "My Aunt Sallie, Mother's youngest sister, moved in to take care of me. Aunt Sallie was only a teenager herself then, and I suppose I took advantage of the fact that she was so young. She tried to teach me sewing and needlework, but when I didn't want to learn, she just let it go, rather than argue with me. With Aunt Sallie, I always felt loved." Elizabeth paused, thinking. "I've often

44

wondered what happened to her, she disappeared suddenly when I was twelve. That was eight years ago. Sometimes I wondered if I'd done something to cause her to go, but I couldn't think of a thing I'd done wrong, and she'd always gotten along well with Papa.''

Mrs. Clarke looked puzzled. ''You mean she left without a word?''

Elizabeth nodded. ''Yes, and then Papa wrote to his first cousin, Agatha, in New Hampshire. She is the spinster of the family. Right away, she came to look after me, but Cousin Agatha and I didn't get along at all. She wanted me to learn to do everything Aunt Sallie had tried to teach me—the sewing and such—but I was rebellious. After a year of emotional turmoil, my father finally sent her back to New Hampshire and told me as long as I kept up with my school work and helped him with his practice, he didn't care if I never learned to sew.

''We were much happier, just the two of us, plus Hattie, the hired lady, who did the cooking and housekeeping. Of course, Cousin Agatha took it upon herself to move in with us for several weeks before my wedding so I'd have a properly formal affair. She was aghast when she realized I *still* hadn't learned much about sewing!''

''I'll be glad to help you learn, Elizabeth. We'll go to the mercantile in Upper Saginaw for supplies,'' Mrs. Clarke offered. ''Several yards of flannel would do well for diapers, a kimono, and light blankets.''

''I'd like that,'' Elizabeth answered, then sipped the last of her tea.

Mrs. Clarke refilled Elizabeth's cup. As she returned to her place at the table, she asked, ''Have you or Jacob seen Mr. Tyler lately?''

Elizabeth thought a moment. ''I haven't seen him, and Jacob hasn't mentioned seeing him either. Why?''

''His wife says he's off hunting, but he never goes

for days at a time. He's not that ambitious. I think he's in the cabin. Sick, maybe," Mrs. Clarke conjectured.

A sharp rap on Mrs. Clarke's door interrupted them.

Mrs. Clarke opened her door to a frightened Mrs. Tyler, and her toddler son.

"Louisa, come in. What is it?" Mrs. Clarke put her arm about the young woman's waist and ushered her inside.

"Pardon, but my husband's deathly ill," she sobbed, deep circles beneath her eyes giving her a haggard expression. "He's been sick for several days, but he wouldn't let me get help. Especially not from 'no lady doctor,' as he put it." She glanced at Elizabeth. "But now . . . *please* come. I'm afraid I'm gonna lose him!"

CHAPTER 4

ELIZABETH AND MRS. CLARKE hurried with Louisa to her cabin. When they reached Mr. Tyler's side, Elizabeth knew he was dead.

After looking him over carefully, Elizabeth spoke. "He died of smallpox. I'm sure of it." She draped a cover over his body.

Louisa whimpered softly, crying into her apron.

Mrs. Clarke comforted the grieving widow. "Louisa, let Elizabeth call the others together and tell them. I'll stay with you awhile, if you like."

Louisa nodded.

As Elizabeth hurried along the path, she thought about the Tylers. The cabin she had just left was small and windowless. Mr. Tyler had not even bothered to lay plank flooring over the dirt. Elizabeth thought about Jacob, and thanked God for her loving, kind husband.

What would become of Louisa and her small child, alone to fend for themselves in the wild settlement? Elizabeth hoped they had relatives to whom they could turn. With her small son to care for, she would have a tough time doing both a man's and a woman's work.

Jacob was the first to answer the bell Elizabeth rang outside the blockhouse door. "What is it? Is someone hurt?"

Elizabeth shook her head. "Worse than that, I'm afraid."

Will hurried to join them. "Was there an accident?" he asked, nearly out of breath.

"No, Uncle Will," Elizabeth answered, "no accident. Mr. Tyler died of smallpox."

Jacob shook his head slowly. "If anyone should have had that vaccination, he should have."

Will removed his cap and slapped it against his thigh in frustration. "I knew it, I just knew something like that would happen. Jacob, we'd better organize the others, some to make the coffin, others to dig the grave."

Residents began to gather. Elizabeth spoke to Will and Jacob. "Will you let the others know what happened? I'll tell Louisa you're making burial preparations. Mrs. Clarke is staying with her, but I'd better get back. She'll have to get the Reverend from the Indian village."

Elizabeth returned to the Tylers to stay with Louisa while Mrs. Clarke went for her husband at the Chippewa camp. Two men came for the corpse, and Elizabeth had just convinced Louisa and her son to rest when a soft knock came at the door. Louisa started to get up. Her son had already fallen asleep beside her, and Elizabeth feared she would waken him.

"You stay put. I'll answer that," Elizabeth said quietly.

Louisa nodded and sank back on the bed.

Mrs. Langton stood outside the door and beckoned to Elizabeth to join her. The other women of the village were with her, and gathered around them.

Mrs. Langton spoke softly. "We've been talking, and wonder if we should take turns staying with Louisa, and bringing her and her little boy their meals."

"Yes, that's a kind and generous offer," Elizabeth responded. "Mrs. Clarke went for her husband. I'm sure he'll want to stay with Louisa for a while, then someone can spell him."

"The men want to know if they should plan to bury Mr. Tyler tomorrow afternoon. Would you ask Louisa and the Reverend if that's all right, then let me know?" Mrs. Langton asked.

"Certainly. I'll come see you when it's all decided," Elizabeth promised.

Mrs. Langton organized the women in the community into shifts to stay with Louisa, and to make sure meals were brought in on a regular schedule. By the following noon, the men had prepared the coffin and gravesite, and the women had cooked a dinner to serve after the funeral.

The next day, Elizabeth spent hours preparing the chowder Mrs. Clarke had taught her to make. It was the same recipe Mrs. Langton had used for the soup she had brought Elizabeth and Jacob on their first night in Riverton, and Uncle Will seemed particularly fond of the dish.

Elizabeth cleaned a pike she had bought from the Indians, minced herbs, which she gathered from the forest, then watched the pot as the soup simmered for hours.

That evening, Elizabeth took supper to Louisa Tyler. Outside Louisa's cabin, Will was splitting wood, arranging it in a neat pile. He beckoned Elizabeth over.

"I feel bad for the lady, Elizabeth. Tyler didn't appreciate her. He didn't even leave enough firewood to last her a week, the lazy bum." He brought his ax down with extra force against the chopping block.

"You're kindhearted, Uncle Will," Elizabeth commented.

Will eyed her pot. "What's in there?"

"Chowder." Will's eyebrow arched with interest.

"There's plenty for you, Louisa, and her boy," Elizabeth commented.

Elizabeth knocked softly on the cabin door, and Louisa answered. She was surprised at the unusual sight that met her eyes. Louisa no longer looked bedraggled as she had the day before. She had brushed her hair neatly into a simple twist at the back. A modest black frock sewn from broadcloth replaced her patched calico dress. Elizabeth caught herself staring.

"Won't you come in," Louisa invited.

Elizabeth stepped forward onto wood this time, instead of dirt, and noticed then that someone had begun to install puncheon flooring. At the back of the cabin, light filtered through a newly installed six-paned glass window. Before she could stop herself, she looked questioningly into Louisa's face.

"Mr. Morgan—Will—added the window and started to lay flooring for me today," she explained. "I'm so grateful to him, and the others who have brought food and visited with Jeremy and me."

Elizabeth couldn't help but wonder if there was more to Will's helping Louisa than concern for a new widow. She handed Louisa the kettle of soup. "I've brought a pot of fish chowder for your supper."

Louisa took it by the handle and set it on the table, then lifted the lid. "Mm. Thank you." Then, as she looked at Elizabeth, her eyes watered, and tears ran down her cheeks.

"What is it, Louisa? What's the matter?" Elizabeth put her arm about Louisa's shoulders.

"I'll never be able to repay you," she sobbed. "You protected Jeremy and me from the smallpox. We'd have surely caught it if it weren't for your vaccinations. And you've been so kind to me since my husband died." She withdrew a hanky from her apron pocket and blew her nose. "How can I ever return the kindness?"

"Some day," Elizabeth smiled, "there'll be something I'll need—a favor perhaps, and I'll be sure to let you know."

Louisa smiled weakly. "I'll be glad to help you out anytime, Elizabeth. You're a true friend."

As Elizabeth continued to call on Louisa throughout the next several days, she noticed a healthy stack of firewood had appeared near Louisa's door, and full buckets of water always stood ready just inside. Coincidentally, Uncle Will had joined her and Jacob much less frequently for dinner or supper, and Elizabeth suspected the newly widowed Louisa Tyler was the reason why.

A week after the funeral, in the heat of a mid-August day, Elizabeth and Mrs. Clarke made their way to Upper Saginaw, walking two miles along the riverbank in the afternoon sun. They followed a well-worn Indian trail to the settlement south of Riverton.

As Elizabeth stepped into the general merchandise store, a young, dark haired clerk greeted her cordially. "What can I do for you, miss?" he asked, flashing a broad smile her way. "Don't believe I've seen you in here before, have I?"

Mrs. Clarke stepped beside her. "Gordon, this is my good friend, Mrs. Jacob Morgan. She and her husband have been our neighbors in Riverton for over a month now."

Color invaded the young man's cheeks. "Ah. New to the valley, then. Welcome, Mrs. Morgan."

"Thank you," Elizabeth replied, suppressing a grin.

Mrs. Clarke eyed the yard goods on the shelf behind the counter. "Gordon, is your mother around? We'd like her to measure some piece goods."

51

"Sure 'nuff, Mrs. Clarke. She's in the back room. I'll get her."

A moment later, a middle-aged woman whose dark hair was pulled into a tight bun at the back of her neck, came to wait on them.

"Well, well, Mrs. Clarke, how are you?" she gushed. "How are things in Riverton? I haven't seen you in . . . I can't remember when."

"Hello, Olive. I'd like you to meet my new neighbor, Elizabeth Morgan. She and her husband, Jacob, moved into the LaMore cabin."

"Oh, how wonderful!" Olive's eyebrows arched, then fell precipitously as the woman leaned over the counter and spoke in a subdued tone. "Tell me, Mrs. Clarke, is it true, what I heard about that Tyler family?"

"Why, I don't know Olive, what did you hear?" Mrs. Clarke asked.

"That," the woman paused to look around, and seeing no one within earshot, continued, "that Tyler fellow caught smallpox from those Indians and died, leaving his wife and child so destitute, they can barely survive."

"Only half of what you say is true," Mrs. Clarke paused, causing Olive's eyebrows to arch even higher than before, "Louisa Tyler's husband did die of smallpox, but she and her son, Jeremy, most certainly aren't destitute. Riverton folk wouldn't let one of their neighbors go wanting."

"And I suppose that Will Morgan is the reason why," Olive conjectured.

"He has done quite a bit for her, but others have helped out too," Mrs. Clarke observed.

"Well," Olive said with a huff, "just you wait until that Will Morgan comes in here again. I'll give him the what-for."

"Oh?"

"He denied he'd spent any time with her when he

52

was in here yesterday, you see. Someone else came in last week, saying she thought there'd be a wedding before first snowfall in your town, and naming Louisa Tyler and Will Morgan as the likely couple. Of course, I didn't believe the woman, especially after Will came by yesterday and swore he hadn't been seeing the widow. You sure they haven't hired your husband to marry them?"

"Now, Olive, she's only been a widow for one week. It's a little early for her to be considering remarrying, don't you think?"

"I suppose so," she sighed.

"Now, if you'd be so kind as to show Elizabeth that bolt of white flannel." She pointed to the yard goods shelved behind the counter.

"Oh, of course." Olive unrolled a length across the counter. "Good and thick. Sure would keep a body warm during cold nights," she commented.

Elizabeth ran her fingers over the material, imagining the soft cloth cushioning the bottom of a newborn infant. "You're right," she agreed. "It will be perfect. I'd like—" she glanced quickly at Mrs. Clarke "—five yards, please." Mrs. Clarke nodded.

"Five yards it is," Olive said, laying a measuring stick atop the fabric.

As Olive's scissors snipped through the soft flannel, Elizabeth picked out embroidery hoops, a needle, and pink and blue floss. She set them on the counter.

When Olive had folded her piece goods neatly, she asked, "Will you be needing thread to go with this, Mrs. Morgan?"

"I'd better take two spools," she answered.

Olive set the white thread with her other merchandise and turned to Mrs. Clarke. "And what can I get for you, Mrs. Clarke?"

"I'd like some tea, and a cone of sugar," she answered.

"My, 'tisn't often we sell a cone of sugar," Olive observed.

"You probably think I'm a spendthrift, but Ben's birthday is coming up, and I so wanted to bake his favorite cake with white sugar, instead of maple. Can you keep my secret, Olive?"

The woman ran her finger across her lips. "My lips are sealed," she assured her.

As Elizabeth and Mrs. Clarke walked the trail back to Riverton, they chatted about the store and its owner. "I couldn't quite understand why Olive seemed so eager to know about Uncle Will and Louisa Tyler."

Mrs. Clarke grinned. "You haven't met Olive's daughter, Priscilla, yet. I suspect she'd like to push your Uncle Will in her direction."

"What's Priscilla like? Is she pretty?"

Mrs. Clarke shook her head. "I couldn't call her that. She's quite shy. Hardly says two words when she sees you. I suspect she's thoroughly dominated by her mother."

The next day, Mrs. Clarke showed Elizabeth how to cut out her baby kimono and piece it together. Then, with the embroidery hoops and floss, she taught her how to cross stitch a pattern onto the material by counting the number of threads in the weave.

After several days of sewing and embroidering, Elizabeth decided it was time to tell Jacob about the baby. She sought Louisa's help. Though Uncle Will had been eating supper with her and Jacob less often, he sometimes joined them unexpectedly, and Elizabeth wanted to be certain he would not be coming tonight.

When Elizabeth knocked on Louisa's door, the widow invited her inside for a cup of herbal tea. As Jeremy came running at a toddler's pace to greet her, she noticed that the dirt floor had entirely disappeared beneath a layer of puncheon flooring, and that both Louisa and Jeremy appeared cheerful and well adjusted.

"Are you sure it's no imposition inviting Uncle Will for supper tonight, Louisa?" Elizabeth sat at a small table in front of the fireplace as she sipped tea. "I'd just like an evening alone with Jacob, so we can discuss some things."

"No trouble, Elizabeth, I'm glad to do it, and happy to return one kindness for the dozens you've shown me."

"Thanks, Louisa, I sure appreciate it."

Louisa smiled as she winked. "I understand your wantin' to have the evening to yourself. I remember times like that when my husband and I were first married." Her eyes watered. "We were happy then, before . . . he started drinkin' so much." Louisa sniffed, then forced a smile to brighten her face. "You enjoy your evening."

"Thanks, Louisa, I will."

Now that Elizabeth knew for a certainty Uncle Will wouldn't be showing up unannounced for supper, she made a special effort to set the mood to tell Jacob about the baby. He had been working late, longer than his uncle for the past several evenings, so she would have plenty of time to prepare before he came home.

After she had set the table and stirred the beans one last time, Elizabeth went to her trunk and took out the kimono and diapers she had made. She hung them over the back of Jacob's chair, then seated herself in front of the fire to hem another diaper.

Several times she got up to move the pot of beans further from the fire, and look out the window. The rumble of thunder portended a storm. Eventually, she had worked all the way around the diaper, yet Jacob had not come home, and Elizabeth began to worry. She laid the newly hemmed diaper with the others over Jacob's chair, then checked the bean pot one last time before moving it off to the side of the fire to keep warm. Taking the lantern from the wall, she decided to look for her husband.

Dusk had fallen, and with it came the inevitable hordes of mosquitoes and damp, chilly air. Elizabeth swatted constantly at the insects buzzing about her face. She hurried along the path toward the land Jacob had been clearing. Her route took her past the blockhouse and dock, where she hesitated, wondering if she should look for Jacob inside the blockhouse.

She approached the heavy door and lifted the latch. As she swung the door open, she held the lantern high, looking around the ground floor, then at the loft.

"Hello, anybody there?" she called. A muffled noise made her curious, and she stepped inside to take a better look.

"Hello," she called again. She heard a scratching sound, then a whoosh from behind as something brushed across her shoulders! Heart racing, she turned to run out the door. As she did, she caught sight of an owl returning to the loft clutching its prey, a mouse. "Hmph. You sure startled me," she said aloud. Elizabeth looked up toward the loft, but could find nothing. She stepped outside and bolted the door shut. Looking up at the bell, she considered sounding the emergency alarm, but decided against it until she had looked farther along the path.

A hazy moon cast little light into the forest around her. White pines towered over Elizabeth, rustling in the breeze. Gusts of wind sent shadows swaying to darken her path as thunder rumbled in the distance. She headed toward the lot Jacob had bought from Uncle Will. Time and again, Jacob had warned her not to go there because of the danger of falling limbs and trees, but she could hear no axes chopping.

She had reached the edge of the lot when a bolt of lightning sent a white shaft of light from the sky, brightening the area ahead of her as if it were daytime. Deafening thunder cracked in the air. Horrified, Elizabeth watched as the wide trunk of a tall white pine on the opposite edge of the clearing split in two, creaking and groaning. In the second that the lightning struck, Elizabeth was shocked at another discovery. The bright light had clearly illuminated the frame structure of a house!

Rain splattered against her face, and Elizabeth knew that there was no time to wonder about the house being built on the lot she and Jacob owned, she must find her husband. With her lantern to guide her, she moved toward the unfinished structure. "Jacob, are you here?" she called, but heard no answer.

She moved in the direction of the split tree, not knowing why, only knowing her instincts drew her there. The rain began falling harder, soaking her shoulders, turning the ground into mud. "Jacob!" she called out. Suddenly, she stubbed her toe and began to stumble, but caught her balance and managed to stay upright. Her scream rent the air as the light of the swinging lantern showed her Jacob's motionless form on the cold, wet ground.

She knelt beside him. "Jacob!" She lifted his head to her lap. "Oh, Jacob, answer me!" she demanded, slapping his cheek, but he did not respond. She checked his breathing. "Thank the Lord, you're still alive," she cried, as his warm breath brushed her skin. "Jacob, you've got to wake up," she sobbed. She had begun to wonder how she would get him to the cabin when two strong hands gripped her shoulders making her shriek with fright. "Let me go!" she shouted, wrenching away. Jacob's head slipped from her lap as she rose, arms flailing. Suddenly, her captor's grip loosened, and she spun to face him.

Brother-of-the-Wolf spoke calmly. "I help lady doctor."

"No! Get away!" Elizabeth shouted. She had not seen Brother-of-the-Wolf since the night he had wrought destruction inside their cabin, but she would never forget her terror.

More firmly, Brother-of-the-Wolf repeated, "I help

57

lady doctor." He bent over Jacob, then Elizabeth tried to push him away. Brother-of-the-Wolf firmly but carefully moved her aside, then gently lifted Jacob in his arms.

Elizabeth trotted behind Brother-of-the-Wolf to keep up as he strode the forest path toward the cabin. Rain streamed down her face, and her soaked clothes clung to her, making her shiver. At last, they stepped inside the cabin door. Brother-of-the-Wolf laid Jacob on the bed. Elizabeth bent over her husband, trying to wipe the moisture from his face with her wet hand.

She straightened quickly, took a dry towel from one wall peg, and his nightshirt from another, then began to dry Jacob off. So intent was she on attending her husband, that several minutes had passed before she realized that Brother-of-the-Wolf had remained, and had stoked the fire, adding warmth to the cabin. When she had exchanged Jacob's wet clothes for his nightshirt, and had covered him with a warm, dry quilt, Elizabeth pulled a chair alongside the bed and held Jacob's hand in hers. Her head bowed, she shut her eyes, and prayed silently for a few moments. Elizabeth could hear Brother-of-the-Wolf stirring in the cabin. When she opened her eyes, he held her Bible out to her.

Puzzled, she took the book, then set it in her lap. The Indian remained beside her, as if waiting for something. Elizabeth remembered then that she had not even thanked him for his help. "Thank you for carrying my husband home," she told him, then looked away, not knowing what else to say.

Brother-of-the-Wolf hunkered down beside her, looking at the unopened Bible on her lap. At last, he spoke. "Pastor Ben teach Brother-of-the-Wolf from Good Book. Now, Brother-of-the-Wolf no drink alcohol. Brother-of-the-Wolf sorry for what he did when drunk. Lady doctor saved Indians from smallpox, but Brother-of-the-Wolf repaid kindness with violence.

Brother-of-the-Wolf was wrong. He ask lady doctor's forgiveness."

"You have my forgiveness," Elizabeth answered, "but have you asked God's forgiveness?"

Brother-of-the-Wolf nodded. "In times past, Brother-of-the-Wolf asked forgiveness of Gitchie Manitou, the Great Spirit of the Chippewas. Now, Brother-of-the-Wolf asks Father God. In times past, Brother-of-the-Wolf walked with Gitchie Manitou. Now Brother-of-the-Wolf walks with Father God."

Elizabeth smiled as she told him, "You've come a long way in learning about God, Brother-of-the-Wolf. I'll pray for you, that you always walk with Father God."

Brother-of-the-Wolf nodded. Slowly, he rose and left the cabin. Elizabeth sensed a peace about Brother-of-the-Wolf, and thanked the Lord that he had given up alcohol.

Soon after the Indian left, Elizabeth tucked the quilt more snuggly about Jacob, then changed out of her wet clothes and hung them to dry. In her nightdress and wrapper, she sat beside her husband throughout the night. She prayed again and again that God would heal Jacob. Falling half-asleep, she pictured herself once more at the lot her husband had bought from Uncle Will, struggling to find Jacob as the storm whipped up around her. When the lightning struck, she saw clearly in her mind the pitched frame of a house roof rising in the sky. She awoke with a start, then realized she had been dreaming. But the house rising in the darkness had not been a dream. She had seen it herself.

Elizabeth leaned over Jacob. He had not stirred. She took his hand in her own once again and brought it to her cheek. "Why, Jacob? Why are you building a house? You didn't even tell me."

She held his hand in her lap as she thought about all that had happened since Jacob had brought her to this wild land. His initial disappointment in Riverton had vanished quickly, replaced by a wave of enthusiasm for the settlement his uncle had started. Perhaps he wanted to stay on in Michigan more than she had realized.

Jacob had promised weeks ago to take her out of the Saginaw Valley come fall, but had he decided they would stay permanently, and not told her?

Elizabeth admitted to herself that, after her early protestations about the place, she had begun to adjust to the pioneer life and the friends and neighbors who shared her struggles. Sure, she would miss the Clarkes, and Louisa too, if she were to leave. But things had changed. She was pregnant. "I can't have a baby here in the wilderness," Elizabeth whispered to herself. Jacob had kept the house a secret from her, but she had kept her own secret by not telling him about the baby.

Elizabeth dozed off. Hours later, as light streamed in the east windows, she awoke to find Jacob propped up on his elbow, staring at her. She leaned over to kiss him.

Moments later, as they lay side by side, he asked, "What happened, anyway? I seem to have lost part of my memory. I was working late at the . . . lot Uncle Will and I were clearing, and a storm came up. I remember thinking I should run for the cabin, or I'd get soaked, when everything went . . . black, or did it explode? I'm having a hard time deciding."

Elizabeth pulled her husband close and kissed his cheek, his forehead, his nose, his chin, then nestled in his arms, her head against his chest. "Oh, Jacob, I was so worried about you. When you didn't come home for dinner, I went looking for you. I went to the lot, and found you next to a tree that had been split open by lightning. Brother-of-the-Wolf carried you home. Jacob, I'm so glad you're going to be all right." She hugged his neck.

Jacob squeezed her tight, then leaned away, a thoughtful look on his face. "You found me at the lot, then you must know about . . ."

"The house," she finished for him. "Jacob," she began slowly, "when we first came here, you said you'd take me back to New York this fall, and now I find out you're building a house. Why didn't you tell me?"

"Elizabeth, I was going to tell you, believe me."

"When, Jacob? When it was all finished? Why didn't you tell me before you started?"

"I wanted to, but Uncle Will—"

"Uncle Will!" Elizabeth scrambled off the bed and paced across the cabin floor. "So that's it. You've been taking your Uncle Will's great advice again. I should have known." She paced some more, stopping behind Jacob's chair, staring at the diapers and kimono she had laid there last night. Picking them up, she fought back the tears that stung her eyes when she thought about having her first baby in the remote settlement of Riverton.

Jacob got out of bed and came toward her on wobbly knees. When his footsteps faltered, she laid down the baby clothes and hurried to his side to prop him up.

"I must have twisted my leg when I fell last night," he said, holding his right knee.

Elizabeth helped him to his chair. She meant to move away then, but he pulled her onto his left knee before she could stop him. She sat rigidly and refused to look at him as he talked.

"Elizabeth, I love you and want only the best for you. There are so many good opportunities for us here, that's why I want to stay in Riverton. We can always sell the house for a good profit come spring, if you still want to leave."

"First it's a few days, then it's in the fall, and now it's come spring." She stared at the floor. "You don't expect me to believe you, after all that, do you Jacob?" She strained against his hold on her.

"No, I suppose not," he answered.

He released her and she walked toward the fireplace, thinking. She wanted to go back to New York so very much, but if she did, she realized now that it would be a journey she would have to make alone. Left behind would be the man she loved, the father of her child, and the home he would provide for them.

She could hear Jacob limping toward her. As he reached her, she turned to face him. Propping himself against the fireplace with one hand, he held out the baby kimono with the other. "For *our* child?"

She took the kimono from him and nodded, her eyes sparkling with unshed tears.

Jacob let out a whoop. "I'm going to be a father!" He hugged Elizabeth with both arms, crushing her against him, and nearly losing his balance in the process.

She held him steady, but was unable to share his joy. Though she was thankful to feel his strong embrace, to know that except for his wrenched leg, he was all right, she was still disappointed that Jacob hadn't told her about the house. She turned him toward the bed, saying, "That's enough excitement for one day. You'd better take it easy for a while, don't you think?"

He sat on the edge of the bed, patted the seat of the chair where she had spent the night, and said, "Elizabeth, sit down. We need to finish talking." She sat down and folded her hands in her lap. He leaned forward, enveloping her hands in his. "Elizabeth, I know that our new house isn't going to be a home unless we fill it with our shared love. Can you forgive me for not consulting you before building?"

Elizabeth searched the face of the man she loved, a man who had escaped a close brush with death last night while trying to build a home for her. When she did not answer right away, a look of pure anguish stole over his features. Then she spoke to him, her tender voice almost a murmur. "Yes, Jacob, I forgive you." She swallowed hard past the lump of emotion in her throat, and went on. "But please promise me that the next time you want to invest in something, you'll let me know."

Jacob traced her cheekbone with his finger as if trying to wipe away the hurt look he saw on her face. "I will, Elizabeth. You have my promise."

Elizabeth did not doubt the sincerity of her husband's intentions, but she did wonder whether or not his promise would hold up under the influence of his uncle.

CHAPTER 5

JACOB STAYED OFF HIS FEET for a few days, giving his knee a chance to heal. It gave them a chance to read old magazines his uncle had lent them, and talk away the hours. Sometimes their talks were lighthearted and funny, at other times, serious and loving. They spent many hours sharing their hopes and dreams for the future.

As they lingered over coffee one morning, Jacob talked at length about the house he was building for his wife. "It's going to be the only frame house this side of Upper Saginaw, and you can bet it will be the best for miles around. When Uncle Will and I are through putting up the frame, I'm going to hire the best carpenter from Detroit to come up here and finish the interior. Uncle Will knows someone who can do fancy wood carving, too. I'll hire him to make you the prettiest bannister you ever saw."

"As for furniture," he went on eagerly, "we'll pick out the finest Detroit has to offer and have it shipped up here on Captain Winthrop's steamer. Your father was kind to offer us his old pieces, but I won't have you using hand-me-downs from New York. Nothing but the best will do for my wife."

Elizabeth's brow furrowed. Her father had told Jacob and her before their wedding that he would ship them furniture he no longer needed whenever they were ready. Evidently, Jacob had decided that used furniture was not good enough. "This all sounds very expensive, Jacob. Are you certain your endowment is large enough?"

He reached across the table and folded Elizabeth's hand in his. "You let me worry about that, Elizabeth. You have enough to think about with the baby on the way."

Now that Elizabeth knew about the house, she was interested in every aspect of its planning, and she trusted Jacob was keeping a complete accounting of the expenditures. Nevertheless, she could not keep from cautioning him. "Please, Jacob, don't get so carried away that you have to borrow money. Papa always believed in paying cash, and so do I."

"Stop worrying. I won't have to borrow," he assured her.

On the fourth day after Jacob's accident, when his knee had improved sufficiently, he went to work on the house, but his day was cut short by rain. While Elizabeth prepared supper, he sat at the table, accounting ledger spread before him, going over figures. Though Elizabeth was extremely curious to see the balance sheets, she knew she must refrain from asking to look at them. When dinner was ready, he cleared his paperwork from the table, returning his ledger to his valise. He did not comment once on finances throughout the meal.

The thunder, which had rumbled before supper, had developed into a full-fledged storm by the time they finished eating, and rain fell in sheets against the shake roof. Jacob, evidently finished with his accounting chores, sat at the table reading while Elizabeth put away their supper dishes. When she had finished, he asked her to join him.

"There's something I'd like to discuss with you, Elizabeth," he said, laying aside an old copy of *The Cabinet of Natural History and American Rural Sports,* that Uncle Will had lent him.

When Elizabeth folded her hands on the table in front of her, Jacob covered them with his own. "What's on your mind, Jacob? From the tone of your voice, it sounds serious. Is there a problem with the house?"

Jacob shook his head. "No. We're a little behind because of my accident, and now the rain, but we'll catch up once the sun shines again. There's something else on my mind, an idea I'd like you to hear me out on."

"Go ahead, I'm listening," she urged.

Jacob squeezed her hands. "Remember when we first arrived here at Riverton, and Uncle Will talked about a bank, and buying land?"

The scene flashed through her mind as if it had been yesterday rather than over a month ago, and a stab of anxiety pierced her heart. "I remember. Go on."

"Well, Uncle Will and I have been talking, and he thinks we'd be foolish not to start a bank here."

Elizabeth pulled her hands away. "And I think you'd be foolish to do so, Jacob," she blurted out, then chewed anxiously on her lower lip. She should have found a better way of telling him how she felt, especially since he had kept his promise to consult her on investments.

He continued, "There are several men over in Upper Saginaw who disagree with you, Elizabeth. They said if they had the chance, they'd get in on a bank."

"But surely we should see that our house is paid for first, Jacob." She tried to stay calm, but her voice wavered. The idea of investing in a bank had upset her when she had heard about it the first time. Discussing it again brought back an unexplainable feeling of panic.

"Elizabeth, if I invest in a bank, one day I'll be able to afford much more than that house. I can't pass up an opportunity for us to be rich!"

"I know you'd like to make the most of the endowment your father gave you, and I realize that without it, we couldn't afford to start building a house right away, but I think you'd be making a big mistake by risking money as Uncle Will proposes." She took an anxious breath. At least she had aired her honest feelings about the subject.

A muscle flexed in Jacob's jaw. "My father and Uncle Will took that risk when they started the bank in Stockport, and they've been pretty successful, haven't they?"

Elizabeth nodded with a quick jerk. "Yes, of course they have." She wanted to remind him that they had other considerations—a house to pay for, a child on the way. . . .

Jacob shoved his chair back. "Elizabeth, the banking rules here are founded on the same principles that made the East grow and flourish. Given half a chance, it will work in the Midwest!" He walked across the floor, reached for his valise from beneath the bed, and lifted his umbrella from a wall peg, then headed toward the door. "I'm going to talk to Uncle Will."

"Jacob, please don't go out in the storm," Elizabeth pleaded.

The thunder grew louder as he opened the door and unfolded his umbrella. Torrents of rain hit the ground, and a puddle swelled outside the door. "I'll be back in a few hours," he told her, then quietly closed the door behind him.

Though Jacob had shut the storm out of the cabin, he could not shut it out of Elizabeth's heart. It seemed

67

like every time a discussion about investments arose, they argued, and her stomach churned at the thought that Jacob might actually invest in a bank. She paced the floor, trying to quell her own fears, telling herself that though he had made one investment without telling her, he would not do the same thing again.

During the next few days, Jacob seemed quiet and withdrawn. He had not brought up the bank issue again, nor had Elizabeth. She sensed a discontentment in Jacob when he was near her, though both seemed satisfied to avoid discussion of the problem.

One morning, a knock came at the door. Louisa and Jeremy stopped by with some sugar cakes, and stayed for tea. Louisa invited Elizabeth and Jacob to join her and Will for dinner the following evening. Elizabeth looked forward to the evening out. She wondered if Will and Louisa might have an announcement to make at the dinner. That evening when she told Jacob of the invitation, she felt he had known it was coming.

"I suspect Louisa and Will have something important on their minds." He got up from the supper table and sat by the fire.

"Did Will ask Louisa to marry him, Jacob?"

Jacob shrugged his shoulders and picked up a book. "I don't know. We'll have to wait till tomorrow to find out."

As the appointed hour approached, Elizabeth fussed with her hair. She had washed it that morning, and pulled it loosely back into a chignon. She could feel Jacob's eyes watching her, and it made her hands tremble as she worked.

Jacob came up behind her and put his hands on her shoulders, turning her toward him. "You look lovely, Elizabeth." With a finger beneath her chin, he lifted her face to press a kiss against her lips.

Elizabeth put her arms around his neck and leaned her head against his shoulder. *Things have gotten back to normal,* she thought. *Maybe he's over the idea of starting a bank.* She felt the tension that had hung between them disappear, and began to relax for the first time in days.

An exuberant Will met them at Louisa's door. "Come in, come on in," he invited, sweeping his arm wide as he stood inside the door. "Louisa, dear, is everything ready?"

Louisa hurried from her place at the hearth. She wore a new calico dress covered with a bright white apron. Her hair was tied back with a periwinkle blue ribbon, and her face beamed more radiantly than Elizabeth could remember. "All set. Come sit down." She took Elizabeth's hands and drew her to the table, which had been set with fresh linen, a bowl of wild flowers in the center, and serving dishes neatly arranged.

When the thick slices of ham, plate of cornbread, and pitcher of maple syrup had been passed around the table, Will spoke up. "Louisa and I have some good news for you."

Elizabeth noticed a stain of pink in Louisa's cheeks as she looked worshipfully at Will. "Go on, Uncle Will, don't keep us waiting. What is it?" she urged.

"Louisa and I," he paused to take Louisa's hand, "have decided to get married."

"How wonderful!" Elizabeth exclaimed. She looked at Jacob, who was wearing a broad grin. "You knew it, didn't you? Will told you ahead of time."

Jacob shook his head firmly. "No, no. Uncle Will never told me he'd asked Louisa to marry him, he just sort of hinted at it."

Louisa reached across the table to touch Elizabeth's arm. "We were wondering if you two would stand up for us. Reverend Clarke's agreed to do the ceremony."

Elizabeth squeezed Louisa's hand. "We'd be honored to. When is the wedding?"

Louisa answered quickly, "Two weeks from Saturday, right down by the river, 'less it's raining. Then we'll have it inside the blockhouse."

Will beamed at his wife-to-be throughout the meal. Whenever he spoke, it was in a tender voice. "Now, dear, how about that special treat I brought you from the store to celebrate."

Louisa nodded. "Why don't you and Jacob step outside for some fresh air while we clear the table," she suggested. "It will be a few minutes."

While Elizabeth helped Louisa, they talked excitedly. "I'm so happy for you, Louisa. I was worried how you'd make out after Zeb died, but I can see I needn't have. You'll soon have a new husband, and Jeremy will have a new daddy!"

"And Will is so fond of Jeremy," Louisa said, "I couldn't have found a better match for us both."

"Speaking of Jeremy, where is he tonight?"

"The Clarkes have him. Said they missed their own grandchildren so much, they'd be glad to watch him. They're even going to keep him the week after Will and I get married so we can take a trip."

"Oh, how wonderful! I didn't realize you had planned a honeymoon."

Louisa corrected her. "It isn't exactly a weddin' trip. More like business. Will said he's got to go to Detroit. He wants to see 'bout startin' a bank here, so he'll need to order some banknotes from the printers."

Elizabeth's stomach churned at the news. She forced her attention on Louisa again, while worrying that Jacob might want to be involved in the trip.

"I suppose Will is going to try to sell some of his land while we're there. I hear tell people are still comin' into Detroit by the thousands." Louisa pulled a plate draped with a napkin from her cupboard, then reached for a canister. "We'll have real coffee tonight sweetened with white sugar, along with a piece of

70

upper shelf gingerbread from Olive Pierce's store." She folded the napkin back for Elizabeth to see the four generous squares of light gingerbread.

"Will has really spent some money on tonight's meal, hasn't he," Elizabeth observed, "with the coffee, white sugar, and light gingerbread, too."

"He surely did, but he claims once he sells his land, we'll build ourselves a mansion and eat upper shelf gingerbread every night. No more of that lower shelf, molasses kind for me!" Louisa measured coffee into the pot and set it over the fire and began to whip the cream. "Why don't you go find the men," she suggested.

When Elizabeth stepped outside, the men were not in sight. She wondered if they had gone for a walk by the river, or to look at the new house. As she neared the blockhouse, she noticed the door stood open. When she approached, she could hear Will and Jacob's conversation.

"Nothing against your wife, Jacob, but she's a little too worrisome. Didn't you tell her how rich she'll be once the bank is set up, and the land sold?"

"I tried to explain it to her, but I don't really think she cares about having more money, Uncle Will. She seems more interested in a home and family."

Elizabeth couldn't believe she was actually standing behind the open door of the blockhouse, listening to a private conversation. She knew she should step inside, but somehow, she couldn't force her legs to move. Guiltily, she remained silent.

"Well," Will paused, "I guess I can understand Elizabeth's concerns, but I still need you to invest. We've got those men in Upper Saginaw all primed for the deal. You're holding things up, nephew."

"I know, I know, and I want to be in on it. It's just that . . . Elizabeth was so against it."

"Well," Uncle Will said thoughtfully, "I suppose there's always that Fenmore fellow from back East.

71

He's dying to invest in this bank. He's a wealthy man too. Started several banks in Connecticut, and is looking for quick profits in the Midwest now. I don't particularly want him in on it, though. He's heading back East before winter, and I wanted investors who were going to be around for a while.''

"I don't want Fenmore in on it either," Jacob agreed, "Still, if I use some of the endowment, I'm going to have to find a way to tell Elizabeth.''

"It's *your* money, Jacob, not Elizabeth's. She knew before she took you for a husband that a married woman doesn't own anything. So it's entirely up to you what you do with that endowment. If you want to spare her some upset, you could wait till you're rollin' in the money, then tell her you put it into starting a bank. When she sees how much better off you are, she'll be glad.''

"I suppose so. I'm burning up to make a big success of myself, you know, especially to show up my brother. He really ridiculed me when I told him I could make a fortune in Michigan.''

"You and he always were in competition, weren't you?''

"Yeah, and by golly, I'm going to prove how wrong he was. I'm going to do it, Uncle Will. Count me in. The deal is on.''

Through the space between the door's hinges, Elizabeth could see the men shaking hands.

"Good. We'll have enough time to set up the deal with the others before the wedding, and then we can take care of the details once we get to Detroit. Why don't you and Elizabeth come? She'd probably like getting away to the city for a few days.''

"I'll have to let you know," Jacob said, moving toward the door.

Elizabeth stepped forward to meet Will and Jacob as they walked out.

"Jacob, Will, I came to tell you dessert is ready,''

she said, hoping neither had noticed the strained tone of her voice.

When they sat down to dessert, Elizabeth wondered how she would make it through the rest of the evening. The upper shelf gingerbread, and her coffee, sweetened with a large lump of white sugar, were tasteless.

Later, when she and Jacob returned home, he seemed more affectionate and talkative than he had in a long time.

"You know, I'm really pleased for Uncle Will and Louisa," he rattled on. "I didn't think much of Louisa when we first moved here, but she's changed a lot since her husband died. She makes Will feel important, and needed." Jacob put on his nightshirt, then reached for Elizabeth, putting his arm around her waist and pulling her close.

Elizabeth wanted to slip out of his embrace, but she remained rigid in his arms and spoke quietly. "Louisa does think a great deal of Will. She says they're going to Detroit on business right after they're married." Elizabeth hoped Jacob would take the opening to tell her about the bank.

"Will mentioned that to me. In fact, he asked if we wouldn't like to come along. You could shop for furniture. The house will be finished enough in a couple of months so we can move into the downstairs," he said, dropping a kiss on her forehead.

Elizabeth pulled back, out of his embrace. "Jacob," her tone was serious, "I heard you and Will talking. I was just outside the blockhouse door when he put the pressure on you to invest in the bank. That's the real reason you want to go to Detroit, isn't it?" A lump rose in her throat.

"Well . . . yes—"

"Jacob, why take such risks when our house isn't finished?"

"Look, Elizabeth. I promised to consult you, but I

never promised to follow your wishes," he stepped close to her, taking hold of her arms. "I'm investing for our future. I was hoping you'd see that."

She wrenched away. "How can you do this to me, Jacob? To us?" Tears stung her eyes as she turned and ran out the door.

CHAPTER 6

ELIZABETH RAN AS FAST as she could toward the river. Out of breath, she slowed to a walk on the path to the site of their new house. Above her, stars twinkled in a wide band across clear midnight skies, and a round yellow moon beamed softly through whispering white pines, lighting her way.

When she reached their new house, she wandered about it, thinking. *What will happen to us if the bank fails? Could I ever forgive him?*

A crackling noise warned her someone was near. She turned and saw Jacob silhouetted in the moonlight, his nightshirt half-tucked into his breeches.

"Elizabeth, I'm sorry. I hate to see you so upset." He stepped beside her, putting his arm about her shoulder.

She shrugged off his touch. "Jacob, can't you understand that what you're doing is tearing us apart? I wanted so much for us to have a happy home, but our house isn't even finished yet, and we can't ever seem to agree."

"We'll be happy, Elizabeth, I'm sure of it. We're

just having a rough time of it right now. Maybe a few days in Detroit will do us both some good."

Elizabeth almost laughed. "If we go to Detroit, I'll be scared the whole time we're there that you'll make another risky investment." She turned her back and wandered to a nearby pine, then leaned against its trunk.

Jacob followed her. "Elizabeth, you're going to have to learn not to worry so much about our investments. Just leave them to me. I only want you to think about our home, and our baby, the two most important things God has given to us."

Elizabeth thought about Jacob's words, and knew he was right. She held out her hand to him.

He took her hand in his, pulling her into his arms. "I love you so much," he whispered against her hair.

"And I love you, Jacob, but I'm scared." She buried her head in his shoulder.

"You needn't be," he assured her. "I'll always be here for you to lean on, no matter what. I promise."

As Elizabeth felt the security of Jacob's arms around her, she prayed this one promise would last forever.

During the next few days, the settlement was abuzz with the news of the upcoming wedding and the plans and preparations to be made. Clara Langton was organizing the ladies for the wedding dinner. Elizabeth found herself sewing a new dress with Mrs. Clarke's guidance.

In spite of the joy that seemed to abound, Elizabeth found her spirits dragging. Each time she thought about Jacob investing in a new bank, she worried that it could fail, and that she would resent him terribly for it. Equally troubling to her was his willingness to involve himself more deeply with Uncle Will, a man whose motives Elizabeth found suspect.

Aside from those concerns, there was the unresolved question of whether she and Jacob would accompany Uncle Will and Louisa to Detroit. Jacob hinted several times that he planned for them to go, but she wondered if she could overcome her resentments and be a good traveling companion on such a trip. She blamed Uncle Will, and didn't feel too kindly toward him. These problems weighed heavily on her mind, and her quiet mood did not escape Mrs. Clarke's attention.

"Elizabeth, is something troubling you?" her neighbor asked, as they sat sewing together one morning at Mrs. Clarke's table.

"It's Jacob," she admitted. "I don't see things his way, and I'm afraid it's caused a problem."

Mrs. Clarke took a deep breath and reached for her Bible. "There's an answer for everything in God's Word. You just have to look for it."

"But how can the Bible tell us what to do today, in 1837? Things are so much more complicated than they were—"

"—in Roman times?" Mrs. Clarke supplied. "It may seem so, but the biblical principles remain the same." She put on her reading glasses and opened the book. "Of course, the first thing we have to establish is your will to follow Christ."

"I've always tried to do that," Elizabeth assured her, "and I think Jacob has too."

"Good," Mrs. Clarke commented, "that means you both believe that the Lord comes first. As for your disagreement," she turned to the New Testament, "in the fifth chapter of Paul's letter to the Ephesians he gave wives some good advice. Why don't you read verses twenty-two through twenty-four." She passed the open Bible to Elizabeth.

"'Wives, submit yourselves unto your own husbands, as unto the Lord. For the husband is the head of the wife, even as Christ is the head of the church: and he is the saviour of the body. Therefore as the church is subject unto Christ, so let the wives be to their own husbands in every thing.'" Elizabeth looked up, puzzled. "But what if I'm sure Jacob is wrong, that he's making a big mistake?"

"Have you discussed the situation thoroughly with him, telling him why you think his decision is wrong?"

"Yes, more than once. And I'm afraid if he does what *he* thinks is right, and it doesn't work out, I'd never forgive him."

"We all need room to make mistakes, and when we do, that's when we need forgiveness more than ever."

Elizabeth was thoughtful. "I never looked at it that way, but you're right."

"I'm sure things will work out one way or another for you and Jacob, as long as you both want to follow Christ."

Late that morning after Elizabeth returned home to prepare dinner, Mrs. Clarke's words kept running through her mind. . . . *things will work out . . . as long as you both want to follow Christ.* Elizabeth had known Jacob for a long time before they were married because he had attended her church, but recently, except for saying grace, she hadn't noticed him praying. She wondered if she had only assumed that Jacob was still putting the Lord first. Right now, it seemed as if he were putting money first.

Her opportunity to ask him came soon after they sat down to eat dinner. He began with the blessing, as usual.

"Heavenly Father, thank you for this nourishment that you have provided. Be with us throughout the day. In Jesus' name, Amen."

"Jacob," Elizabeth began, passing him a bowl of parsley potatoes, "I know you've been praying before every meal to ask God's blessing, but are you still asking Him about other things, too?"

His brows arched as he put several small potatoes on his plate. "As a matter of fact, I am."

"You are?" Elizabeth asked with surprise. "I didn't realize, I mean, lately, I've only heard you pray at the table." She helped herself to some potatoes and passed the smoked pork chops.

"You may not hear me praying, but I do consult God on almost everything," he assured her, helping himself to three chops.

"Even on investing in a bank?" The question slipped out before she could stop it.

"Yes," he stated, setting the platter aside, "even on the bank, and I believe God's given us that opening as a way to help others, by providing financial services."

Elizabeth's mouth dropped open. "I'm really surprised," she admitted, "because I was afraid you were putting money before God's will." She felt uncomfortable questioning Jacob's motive.

His cheeks reddened. "I've told you I prayed about it. Now please, let's not talk about it again." He stabbed hard at a potato, clanking his fork against his plate.

Conversation was strained throughout the rest of the meal. Afterward, Jacob took a nap, while Elizabeth sat at the table sewing. While Jacob slept, Elizabeth thought about Riverton, and how much effort Jacob was putting into making it seem like home to her. She must not fight him on his investments any longer, but must support him in his decisions. He had prayed for God's will and was trying to follow it, and she should no longer question his judgment.

Elizabeth set a tall order for herself, to support Jacob's decisions, regardless that she might not agree with them. She wasn't sure she could live up to her new pledge to herself, but she prayed that God would give her the strength not to contradict her husband.

When Jacob woke up, his mood seemed lighter. He came to the table and sat across from her. "I've got to get back to work soon," he said, leaning across the table, "but I want you to be thinking about Detroit. It will do us good to get away for a while. Make out a list of everything you could possibly want for yourself, our baby, and the new house. We'll enjoy a few days away." He laid his hand on hers. "One more thing, Elizabeth," worry lines creased his forehead as he continued. "I want to tell you about the business I have to take care of while we're in the city."

"I thought you and Uncle Will were going there to see about getting some banknotes printed," Elizabeth conjectured.

"We are, but there's more. I'm going to sell some land while we're there, lots Uncle Will is going to let me have at a very low price."

Elizabeth flinched at the news, but kept her tongue still.

"In order to complete the house and furnish it the way I want, plus invest in the bank, I need to come up with some extra cash. Selling land is the quickest way to increase my capital."

"I hope you'll get a very good price for it, Jacob," Elizabeth said, keeping her voice level. "It would be nice to know that our investments here are increasing in value."

"Yes . . . it would."

Elizabeth could see that her calm response had taken Jacob by surprise, but he recovered quickly.

"Elizabeth, I don't want you to worry for one second about land prices. I only told you I was going to buy the extra lots because I promised to talk to you first about investments. I'm pleased that you aren't upset." He squeezed her hand. "I have to get to work now. I'll see you at suppertime." He got up from the table and headed for the door, but turned back to say again, "I promise you we'll have a great trip to Detroit."

Elizabeth continued her sewing, and thinking.

. . . *I promise you* . . . She had heard those words

before, and they were spoken all too lightly as far as Jacob was concerned, she concluded. She wasn't as certain as Jacob that they would have a great time on their trip. Pushing those concerns aside, she concentrated on the dress she was sewing for Will and Louisa's wedding. There were many exciting preparations to be made for that day.

The following afternoon, the women of Riverton sat around the Clarke's table with Louisa to discuss details of the wedding. Mrs. Langton, apparently an inveterate planner, opened the discussion.

"Do you realize that we are about to make history? Louisa and Will's wedding will be Riverton's very first. We must do everything we can to make it a memorable occasion." Clara Langton's normally brusque approach seemed to have dissolved in a wave of enthusiasm.

Mary Stone looked up from the quilt square she was piecing to comment. "Why, anybody would think 'twas your own daughter, Tess, taking the vows." Tessa Langton, a pretty, but shy fourteen year old blushed.

Louisa spoke up. "I surely appreciate your concern, but you needn't get fancy. Will doesn't want word of the wedding to spread outside Riverton. Otherwise, he says half of Upper Saginaw is bound to show up uninvited. He's promised to provide the venison, and most of the menfolk have already offered to see to the roastin'. All's we need are the trimmings."

Mrs. Langton began again. "The trimmings are the most important part! They make the difference between a meal and a feast. First, there's the cake. It should be an extra fancy one."

Mae Clarke spoke up. "I've got the white sugar, and without our friend, Mrs. Pierce, suspecting about the wedding. She thinks it's only for Ben's birthday."

81

Mrs. Langton continued. "I've got lots of fresh white flour. If you can spare us some eggs from your setting hen, Mary, we'll have a fine confection large enough to serve each Riverton resident a generous piece—though we'll have to cut carefully or it won't go around."

Mary nodded. "Simple enough, Clara. What about the breads and rolls?"

Emma Farrell joined the discussion. "That's my favorite, bakin' bread. I'll do some special sweet rolls along with light and dark loaves."

The Reverend Clarke's large form filled the open doorway. "Pardon me, ladies. I didn't mean to interrupt, but I'd like to speak with my wife and Louisa for a moment."

Mae and Louisa excused themselves, then Mrs. Langton continued. "Now remember, we want everyone out in their Sunday best. I know we don't have much call for putting on our fancy duds, aside from Reverend Clarke's sermon each week, so this will be our chance."

Reverend and Mrs. Clarke and Louisa rejoined the meeting. The Reverend Clarke cleared his throat. "Mrs. Langton, if you don't mind terribly, I'd like a word with you ladies."

"Please, be our guest, Reverend," Clara insisted.

"I have some joyous news to share about our neighbors, Chief Noc-chick-o-my and his people. After many months of preaching to the Chippewas, the Chief has embraced our Christian beliefs, and several heads of household have followed his example."

"Praise the Lord," several murmured.

The Reverend, his kind face beaming with joy, nodded agreement. "I spoke with Will earlier, and now with Louisa, and they've expressed a desire to extend, through me, an invitation to Chief Noc-chick-o-my's village to attend their wedding. I'm hoping you'll make his people feel most welcome." Stunned silence met his announcement. He paused a moment longer. "Now, if you'll excuse me, I must get back to my work at the village." He made his way out.

When the Reverend was several yards down the path leading from the open door, Mrs. Langton began with a rush, "Surely, Louisa, you can't mean to invite those . . . unkempt . . . untidy people to your wedding. They'll ruin—"

"Ruin what, Mrs. Langton?" Louisa cut in, "Your idea of what my wedding ought to be? I'd like very much to have them join the celebration. How will they ever understand our ways, if we shut them out, pretendin' they don't exist? I'd be much prouder to have my weddin' day remembered as the first ceremony to which the Chippewas were formally invited, rather than a time when we chose to exclude them."

Wrinkles creased Mrs. Langton's forehead. "But . . . but . . ." she stuttered, then turned to Elizabeth. "Elizabeth, you've been to their village. You've seen what they're like. Can't you convince Louisa what a mistake she's making?"

"Sorry, but I agree with Louisa. The mistake would be in not inviting them. Think of the Chippewa children, Mrs. Langton. Don't you want them to learn the meaning of a Christian marriage? Don't you want them to see that the ceremony means more than a feast, that it means a promise to be faithful to one chosen love?"

Mrs. Langton's eyes widened. "After what happened to you, with that young Indian breaking your door down and ransacking your cabin, you want to be their friend? I can't believe it!"

"But Mrs. Langton," Elizabeth responded, "Brother-of-the-Wolf apologized for what he did. He believes in God and has stopped drinking alcohol. I hold no grudge against him."

Mary Stone cut in. "I admire Elizabeth," she said,

looking around at each of the other women. "If anyone in Riverton had a reason to want them excluded, surely it is she."

Clara Langton began anew. "Then what about the dinner? We can't be expected to provide for that entire Indian village."

Mrs. Clarke spoke up. "You needn't worry about food. The Chief will see to it that his villagers come laden with plenty to eat. We need only to provide them a place at our tables, and in our hearts."

"Amen," Louisa added.

Silence followed. Finally, Mrs. Langton responded in a subdued tone. "Very well. Since the Chippewas will be coming, we'd best plan the wedding feast accordingly."

And plan they did. Then the work began. Throughout the entire week before the wedding, preparations were underway. Ladies worked on their batter and dough while men constructed tables, dug roasting pits, and set up spits.

Two days before the big event, Elizabeth and Louisa sat together at Louisa's table, putting the finishing touches on their new dresses.

"I never expected such a fuss for our wedding," Louisa commented. "I'd have eloped with Will, if he'd wanted to."

Elizabeth grinned. "I think people want a reason to celebrate. It's a hard life here, Louisa. Though Mrs. Langton and the other ladies don't show it, they are pleased to prepare for such a happy event."

"I suppose you're right," Louisa agreed, "though I hadn't thought of it that way." A frown line appeared at the corner of her mouth.

Elizabeth touched Louisa's hand. "You aren't nervous, are you?"

"Nervous?" Louisa gave an anxious laugh. "No. Guess I'll just be happy to have it done with. There's one thing about it that does worry me, though." She knotted her thread and broke it between her teeth.

"What's that?" Elizabeth asked.

"I got to thinkin' the other night about Mrs. Langton and the Chippewas. I sure hope she doesn't do anything to insult them when they come. I'd hate to have hard feelings come out of our inviting them."

"I don't think we'll have to worry. She seems to realize it's really for the best that we try to improve relations with the Indian village."

"I certainly hope you're right," Louisa said wistfully. "I went over to their village one or two times myself a few months back to trade for some fish. When I saw how those women work and live, I'll tell you, I sure give them credit. Ever since then, I've had a special place in my heart for the Indians." Abruptly, she began on another topic. "Say, did you hear anything about a bear in the settlement the night before last?"

"A bear? No, Jacob hasn't mentioned anything. Why?"

"Well, Mr. Farrell was up here the other day. They live down by the river, you know. He says he heard a terrible tussle just about suppertime a couple nights back. Seems one came along and picked up a hog of his and started carryin' it off. He went to get his rifle an' take a shot at it, but the critter was plumb out o' sight before he could take aim."

"No!" Elizabeth exclaimed. "I never heard of such a thing."

"Seems to me, those bears are a mite hungry to be doin' that, don't you think?"

"I suppose you're right." Elizabeth agreed.

Two days later, when the morning of the wedding arrived, the Farrell's bear problem was the last thing on Elizabeth's mind. An air of excitement stirred in Riverton. The men had worked throughout the night in shifts over the roasting pits. Tables with benches had been erected in the center of the clearing. By the river, a crude altar stood near the blockhouse.

Elizabeth, in her new calico dress, brushed her shiny dark hair away from her face and tucked marsh marigolds behind her ear. As she looked at her image in her hand mirror, she glimpsed Jacob in the background, watching her. She smiled. Things had gone more smoothly between them since she had concentrated on her home, and left worry over investments to Jacob. She had even begun looking forward to their trip to Detroit, as Jacob had suggested.

Jacob came up behind her, outfitted in denim. How informal they looked compared to the attire worn by the attendants at their own wedding in New York only weeks earlier. He took the mirror from her hand and set it aside, then turned her toward him. "Mrs. Morgan, you look lovely indeed." He took her hands in his and brought them to his lips, kissing her fingertips.

"Do you really think so?" she wondered. "This is so different from the silks I remember when we said our vows."

"Life is much more rugged here, too rugged for silks, and you know how informal Uncle Will is. I doubt he could last five minutes in a waistcoat and doublet, if he had them, which I'm sure he does not."

Elizabeth chuckled at the thought. "You're right."

"Are you ready to go? It's time."

Elizabeth kissed Jacob's cheek. "Ready," she said, tucking her hand in his arm.

They mingled with several neighbors in the clearing as they waited for the bride and groom. Will Morgan emerged into the clearing leading a bay gelding, and the wedding procession began. Jacob and Elizabeth walked behind Will, and their neighbors followed as he led the way to Louisa's cabin. The bride stood in her open door, waiting. A white poke bonnet lined with pink roses to match her dress shaded her face.

When Louisa saw the horse, her whole face spread

into a smile of delight. Will lifted his slender bride easily to the horse's back.

The procession continued around the village until the families from every cabin had joined in. Where the north trail entered the settlement, the Indians waited in a long line, falling into step single file behind the Riverton residents.

Soon, the wedding party arrived at the altar by the river. Close behind them, Mae Clarke held little Jeremy's hand. Chief Noc-chick-o-my and his family stood at the very front, beside Mae Clarke and Jeremy.

"We are gathered together," the Reverend Clarke began.

In soft tones, Elizabeth heard Mae's voice translating the entire ceremony into Chippewa for the chief and his family.

At last, the Reverend Clarke introduced the new couple, and they turned to face their guests. A beaming Will kissed Louisa's lips.

A murmur of approval went up from the Chief and family. "Ho, ho. Ho, ho," they said, smiling.

Again, Will lifted Louisa to the horse, then led the wedding guests to the feast.

Soon, the wedding party had settled at the head table, and their Riverton neighbors and Chippewa friends filled in the others.

The wedding guests proceeded to enjoy the feast. Toward the back of the gathering, Elizabeth was glad to see Brother-of-the-Wolf, and recognized his two brothers with him.

When the meal was finished, the men drifted off to talk while Mrs. Langton and her helpers prepared for the cutting of the cake. Louisa and Elizabeth wandered among the guests, giving their Chippewa neighbors a special welcome.

Beloved-of-the-Forest made a special point to express her best wishes to Louisa, and renew her acquaintance with Elizabeth, using a combination of English words she had learned and Mrs. Clarke's translations of her Chippewa. The young woman told them, "I, like my father, believe our villages must help one another. We are honored to share in the celebration of your marriage. You are always welcome in our village, as you have welcomed us into yours."

Mrs. Langton joined them. "It's time to cut the cake, Louisa. You and Will get the first pieces."

Louisa, Elizabeth, and Mrs. Clarke followed Mrs. Langton to the center table where the white wedding cake was displayed. The guests gathered around.

As Will and Louisa prepared to cut the first slice, a startling, raucous noise came from the woods nearby.

Everyone turned in the direction of the noise. A huge black bear stood at the edge of the clearing!

A gasp went up from the assembled guests.

As the bear lumbered toward the table that held the cake, people scattered in fright, running off in all directions.

"Get a rifle!" someone shouted.

Jacob making his way through the crowd to Elizabeth shouted, "Run, Elizabeth! Run!"

Elizabeth froze.

Never before had she seen such a large creature. He stood upright, coming nearer, growling as he came. She stood-stock still, her back to the table, the cake behind her. Mute with shock, she remained paralyzed.

The bear raised his paw and let out a deep, ferocious growl.

Elizabeth squeezed her eyes shut and shielded her face with her arm, resigned to the blow.

The blow never came. Loud, guttural cries went up. Elizabeth opened her eyes in time to see Brother-of-the-Wolf and his two brothers attack the bear with their knives.

The bear wrestled them to the ground, mauling them ferociously. The three braves tumbled, dust and fur flying, as they struggled with the mighty brute. Finally, all was quiet.

Elizabeth slumped into Jacob's strong arms.

CHAPTER 7

ELIZABETH BLINKED SEVERAL TIMES. Finally, Jacob's face came into focus, then the faces of others who crowded around her bed—Louisa, Mae Clarke, Uncle Will. She raised her head from her pillow.

Jacob squeezed her hand. "Rest easy, sweetheart. The bear's gone."

Louisa added, "He's dead. They killed him."

Elizabeth shook her head to clear it. A piece at a time, the incident came back to her. "Brother-of-the-Wolf . . ." Her brows came together as she tried to remember.

Will informed her, "Brother-of-the-Wolf and his two brothers cut that bear down with their knives. Some of their relatives are takin' the bruin to their camp now."

Movement in the open doorway caught Elizabeth's eye, and she saw that Brother-of-the-Wolf was looking in on her. She beckoned to him, but he would not enter. "Please, Brother-of-the-Wolf, come in. I'd like to speak with you."

The brave hesitated, then came forward to sit on his haunches beside Elizabeth's bed.

She placed her hand on his shoulder as she spoke. "I will always remember you, the strong brave who saved my life. May God bless you."

Brother-of-the-Wolf replied timidly. "Kind daughter of white medicine man, you have saved many more lives than I. Today, you received a small reward." He left before Elizabeth could say more.

Mrs. Clarke commented to Elizabeth, "My husband tells me Brother-of-the-Wolf has come to think of you as his sister, and Jacob as his brother."

A pleased look stole over Elizabeth's features. "As God's children, we *are* brothers and sisters."

Jacob brushed his hand over Elizabeth's forehead, "Thank the Lord for our brother."

Elizabeth nodded, then swung her legs off the bed. "Now that I'm feeling better, I'm looking forward to sampling that wedding cake!"

She moved to the door with Jacob supporting her elbow. The others followed. When she stepped outside, she noticed that the center of the village looked as though a tornado had struck. Scattered belongings and overturned tables lay strewn about.

Behind her, Will let out a howl. "Will you look at that! Mrs. Langton's guarding that cake with a corn broom!"

Elizabeth laughed when she saw the crowd of little ones gathered around the one standing table, trying to get a fingerful of frosting.

"Louisa, my wife," Will continued, in a jovial mood, "let's cut the cake for Elizabeth and the rest of our guests so we can be on our way. I've reserved a room for us at the Western House in Upper Saginaw tonight, and we'll have to leave soon."

The following morning, Jacob and Elizabeth met Will and Louisa in Upper Saginaw to board the steamer, the *Governor Marcy*, for the trip to Detroit. After they arrived in the city, they took rooms at the

Woodworth Hotel. The next day, Will and Jacob supplied their wives with some hard cash money for shopping, and went about the business of selling their land.

Groups of men swarmed outside the Detroit land office. Speculators with land to sell, and immigrants so fresh off the steamer from Buffalo they still wore sea legs. Will conferred with Jacob as they stood on the fringe of the crowd. "Pay close attention to what I say, and if I ask you a question, you just agree with me."

Jacob nodded, then followed his Uncle Will through the hordes of people, catching snatches of conversation.

"Grand River Valley, that's the place to settle down. In a few years, it'll be another Rochester . . ."

"Come to Marshall, in the Kalamazoo Valley, the most flourishing village of the peninsula . . ."

They listened for nearly two hours to similar talk, and all the while, Will kept mingling, looking. Suddenly, he spotted someone and stopped short. Jacob nearly collided with him, before he veered off to the left, zeroing in on an immigrant who remained on the fringe. "Good day, sir. Just arrived from back East?"

The stocky man nodded. "We stepped off the *Ohio* just this mornin'. Came from Genesee County, New York."

Will extended his hand. "I'm Will Morgan, and this is my nephew, Jacob Morgan."

The stranger shook their hands in turn. "Isaac Knight. Pleased to meet ya'."

"Well, now, Mr. Knight, I bet you're a blacksmith. Am I correct?"

"I am, at that," he replied.

"I just happen to be looking for a blacksmith, myself."

"Is that right? Don't know as I'd be any good to ya', Mr. Morgan. It'll be some time 'fore I'm established, an' I don't rightly know yet just where that'll be."

"Then Isaac, my good man, providence has struck again. Jacob 'n I have some land up in the Saginaw Valley. Good land, too, including plats in a thriving town. In fact . . ." Will paused to look around, then slipped a map from beneath his shirt and continued in a low voice, "I've been savin' a choice spot for a blacksmith's shop right on Main Street in Riverton."

Isaac Knight watched with interest as Will unfolded the map and pointed out the location. "Hmm. Riverton, you say. That a prairie town? My wife's hankerin' to move to a prairie."

"It's prairie you want? Then prairie we've got, along with some wooded lots for those who prefer otherwise. Isn't that right, Jacob?"

Jacob, stunned by his uncle's outright deception, turned away with a choking cough.

Isaac looked over the map. "How much ya' be wantin' for that lot?"

Will thought a moment, then answered. "Well, Isaac Knight, that depends. You're gonna need more than just a lot for your shop. You're gonna need a place to build your house. Got any children?"

"Yes. Four." he confirmed.

"Any sons?"

"Two. Don't see what difference—"

"Could make you a lot of difference," Will cut in. "Some day, those boys of yours are gonna need land of their own. The way land prices are goin', they won't be able to afford it, 'less you buy it for 'em cheap right now."

"How cheap?"

"How's five dollars an acre sound for fertile farmland, more fertile than the Genesee Valley where you come from?"

Isaac shook his head. "No. Can't do it. At three an acre, I might think on it some."

Will pointed to the map. "Right along in here's a good forty acres. It's on the river and close to town. You pay me hard cash money for it at four dollars an acre, and I'll throw in the lot for your smithy, and one for your house in town, as well."

Isaac arched one bushy brow high. "Now that's surely a temptin' offer."

"And one that won't last long, I can assure you. By the time the week's out, I'll have sold the rest of my land and be on my way back home to the peace and quiet of the Saginaw Valley. Nothin' against Detroit, mind you, but with the crowds comin' in here, it's pure relief to get away, if you know what I mean."

Isaac nodded. "I do, indeed. My wife and I couldn't even get a room. Hear there's not a place in town to be had. She's waiting for me with the young 'uns in front of the Woodworth."

"The Woodworth, you say? That's where we're staying! Come to my room there man, and we'll close the deal so you can catch the *Governor Marcy* right away to Riverton." Will put his arm on Isaac Knight's shoulder and made his way toward the hotel. Jacob followed a few paces behind, still shocked by his uncle's behavior.

That same morning, Elizabeth and Louisa sat in the ladies' parlor of the Woodworth Hotel, sipping tea.

Louisa looked around her with childlike curiosity. "I've never seen a place like this. When Zeb and I came through Detroit last year, we didn't even stop overnight. We couldn't afford to pay for a room. 'Course there weren't any rooms even if we'd *had* some money." She paused, thinking. Her eyes lit as she began again. "Did you notice how quick that clerk changed his story about the place being filled up once Will slipped him a coin?" She chuckled, shaking her head. "My husband's sure somethin', the way he gets things done."

94

Elizabeth didn't agree with Will's way of doing things, but evidently, in Louisa's eyes, he could do no wrong. Elizabeth changed the topic. "What do you say we take a stroll and see what the merchants are showing in their windows?"

"I'd like that. Might even buy me somethin'." She lowered her voice and added, "Will gave me some money before he and Jacob took off this mornin'." She jiggled the little drawstring bag on her wrist.

The front of the Woodworth Hotel was packed with a mélange of humanity, many of them immigrants who could not find lodging. As Elizabeth and Louisa made their way through the crowd, one woman in particular caught her eye. She sat on a trunk, with her blond daughters dressed alike, perhaps six or seven years old, asleep on each side. Stretched out at her feet were two boys who might have been in their early teens. The woman looked up as Elizabeth passed in front of her. With her blond hair caught back in a knot, and her pale blue eyes, she looked almost exactly like Elizabeth's Aunt Sallie, only older than when Elizabeth had last seen her.

Elizabeth hesitated, wondering whether she should speak to the stranger. She smiled, and tiredly, the woman smiled back, but showed no hint of recognition.

Louisa pulled Elizabeth by the arm. "Are you comin'?"

Elizabeth took one last look, then followed Louisa into the bright August sunshine.

"What a glorious day! I do believe I might have myself a little shoppin' spree," Louisa stated, working her way past the crowded shops.

Elizabeth followed Louisa to the milliner's. While Louisa tried on hat after hat, Elizabeth couldn't help wondering if the woman she had seen could be her aunt. She gave up the notion when she realized that the woman's sons were too old to be Aunt Sallie's children. Even if she had married right after leaving Elizabeth and her father, her oldest would be no more then seven, and the oldest lying at the woman's feet was at least thirteen.

True to her word, Louisa did shop all morning long. In each store, she would encourage Elizabeth to buy something too, but Elizabeth held back, saying she would wait until Jacob had time to go with her.

"Jacob's not going to want to spend time lookin' at women's things, for heaven's sakes, Elizabeth. If you want somethin', you'd best get it," Louisa reasoned.

"Maybe tomorrow," Elizabeth hedged. "He might have time then to look at some household goods."

"Have it your way. But don't say I didn't warn ya'!" Carrying packages in both arms, she followed Elizabeth back to the hotel. "Let's sit in the parlor soon as I put these in the room," she suggested.

As Elizabeth stepped in front of the hotel door, she noticed the family of four children and assorted baggage hadn't moved, only this time, all the children were awake, and each of the boys held a little sister on his lap while their mother stretched her legs.

"I'll see you in a few minutes, Louisa," Elizabeth called. Louisa nodded, and headed inside.

The blond woman was combing her daughters' hair, retying their ribbons. Elizabeth's curiosity got the best of her, and she decided that, even though the woman couldn't possibly be her Aunt Sallie, it wouldn't hurt to be friendly. She approached her.

"My, but your daughters surely are lovely. It's easy to see they take after their mother," Elizabeth commented.

"Thank you," the woman answered, looking up. A puzzled look crossed her face, then she turned back to her task.

Hearing such few words, it was hard to tell, but Elizabeth thought the woman's voice sounded familiar. "I hope you don't mind my introducing myself," she continued, "but you remind me so much of my aunt back in New York State. I'm Elizabeth Brownell Morgan." When the woman's eyes met hers, Elizabeth offered her hand.

The stranger's face drained of color. "Elizabeth Brownell? Of Stockport? Then you're my niece!"

"Aunt Sallie!"

Sallie threw her arms around Elizabeth's neck. "Dear girl, how have you been? It's been years!"

"Aunt Sallie, it really is you! I can hardly believe it. I didn't think I'd ever see you again." Elizabeth held her close before stepping back to look at her. "How long has it been?"

"So long, I can hardly remember. My, but you've grown to a beautiful young woman, Elizabeth. I always knew you would." She glanced down at her children. "Elizabeth, meet my children, my stepsons, Todd and Charles, and my daughters, Amy and Sarah."

Stepsons. So that's how Aunt Sallie had become the mother of boys too old to be her own.

Through the open hotel doors, Elizabeth saw Louisa in the lobby and beckoned her to join them.

Joining them, Louisa said, "I looked for you in the parlor, Elizabeth, but when you weren't there, I decided to look in the lobby."

"I'm sorry, Louisa. I've just discovered someone I haven't seen for years." She indicated her aunt. "Aunt Sallie, this is my friend, Louisa Morgan. Louisa, my Aunt Sallie. And these are her children, Todd, Charles, Amy, and Sarah."

Louisa smiled at them. "Such a beautiful family."

Elizabeth explained excitedly, "Aunt Sallie took care of me after my mother died." She turned to her aunt. "Where is your husband? I'd love to meet him."

"He's gone to see about buying some land. Said he'd be back for us in awhile, then we'd be on our way." She squeezed Elizabeth's shoulders. "So much time has passed, I'm sure a lot has happened since I last saw you. I wish we could chat."

Louisa suggested, "Elizabeth, why don't you and your aunt chat in the parlor while I stay here with the children."

"Oh, Louisa! Sure you don't mind?"

"Not a bit. Go on now, enjoy yourselves."

Sallie admonished her children. "Now you behave yourselves for Mrs. Morgan. No arguments, no running out in the street." She turned to Elizabeth. "Let's go catch up on old times."

When they entered the ladies' parlor, they were fortunate to find two unoccupied chairs. Soon, they were served glasses of fruit punch to cool them on the unusually warm September day.

"So tell me, Elizabeth, how is your father?"

"Papa's fine, at least he was well the last time I saw him."

"Good. I'm glad. Elizabeth," she hesitated, "did he ever remarry?"

"Papa? No! I don't think he ever got over Mama's passing. I guess she was his one true love."

Sallie nodded.

Elizabeth leaned forward and squeezed her aunt's wrist. "I wish you could meet my Jacob. We were married in June."

Sallie's brows arched. "Is he here? In the hotel? I would dearly love to meet him, if I could."

"He's tending to business with his Uncle Will. They'll probably finish about supper time, but I suppose you'll be gone by then."

Sallie nodded. "I expect so. Tell me, are you living in Michigan now? It seems odd that we should meet again so far from New York State."

"Jacob and I came out here to live in a town called Riverton, up on the Saginaw River. His uncle had written us and encouraged us to buy land here in

Michigan while it was still cheap. Uncle Will bought several acres at an auction, laid out the town, then convinced Jacob to move out here. He sent us a map before we left New York, showing us what the village was like. There were parks, churches, a school, and plenty of shops all laid out. We were so excited! Only problem was, when we got here, there wasn't any town at all—only a handful of log cabins on the river, and a thick forest all around."

"Oh, no! What did you do?"

"Tried to adjust as best we could. Riverton is very primitive. We're staying in someone else's cabin until our house is finished. There's a whole village of Indians less than a mile away."

Sallie gasped.

"They're friendly, though," Elizabeth assured her. "Uncle Will ate supper with us that first evening, and explained how Riverton would grow fast with all the people moving into the new state, and assured Jacob he could buy land from him and resell it at a big profit. I was against the idea of staying for a long time, but I've adjusted to Riverton now. I can hardly believe I'm even starting to like it there!" Elizabeth sipped from her punch, then asked, "Where are you and your family going to be living?"

Sallie shook her head. "Don't exactly know yet. Isaac just said when he'd closed a deal on some land, we'd be on our way to claim our property. We decided to find something in a prairie town, a village site for his smithy, and maybe some farmland, if we can afford it. I couldn't live in the forest, like you are. Much as I'd enjoy being neighbors, I just couldn't! We've saved every penny for years and years so we could afford to move West and farm prairie land. It's our dream come true." She sipped another swallow of punch, then gazed out the window, thinking.

Elizabeth framed her next question carefully, then interrupted her aunt's thoughts. "Aunt Sallie, why did you leave Papa and me without a word?"

Sallie looked at her, then her eyes dropped. "I was hoping you wouldn't ask me that, Elizabeth, because it's the one question I can't answer," she said uneasily.

"Can't? Or won't?" Elizabeth gently challenged. "I asked myself a hundred times what I'd done to make you go away, but I couldn't think of anything."

"It was your father," she quickly supplied. "I had to go because of your father."

"Papa sent you away? But I never heard a cross word between you!" She continued on in a rush. "Aunt Sallie, after you left us, Papa's Cousin Agatha came to stay with us. She and I argued nearly every day, and Papa didn't fare much better. I saw Papa angry enough to send someone away, and I know that wasn't it with you. Won't you please tell me what made you go?"

"I'm sorry, Elizabeth, I haven't anything more to say on the matter. It's all in the past—"

"But not forgotten."

"Then it should be. Now," she attempted a smile, "I've enjoyed chatting with you, but I really must get back to my children."

"You'll keep in touch, won't you? I'd like to know where it is you settle down. Promise me you'll write me at Pierce's Mercantile in Upper Saginaw."

"I'll try, Elizabeth. Now, I really must go." As she stood, Elizabeth began to rise also, but she motioned her to stay. "You might as well retain your comfortable seat. I'll send Louisa in to join you. I wish you the best, Elizabeth. Goodbye." She stooped to brush Elizabeth's cheek with a kiss, then left without another word.

Hours later, after a fine dinner with their wives, Will and Jacob withdrew to Will's room to talk business, while Elizabeth and Louisa chatted in the other room.

Will plopped on the bed while Jacob sat on the edge of the room's only chair.

"So that's how it's done, my boy. Tomorrow, you're on your own. I bet you'll sell plenty of the lots you bought from me."

Jacob rubbed his chin. "I don't know, Uncle Will. I don't plan to deceive anybody. And how did you know that Knight fellow was a smithy before you even asked him? And what if he hadn't had hard cash? Then where would we be?"

Will sat up. "You've got to be observant, my boy, and develop a sense about these things. Of course, the first priority is money. Your target has to have cash— hard cash, not paper. Can't trust that paper currency, 'less of course, it says Riverton Bank on it like ours is gonna." Will chortled.

"So how'd you know he had hard cash? I didn't exactly see him tossing coins in the air."

"Just as we came upon him, he slipped a leather pouch down inside his shirt. It's a sure sign, my boy, that leather pouch. Keeps those pieces of eight from punching holes in your pockets."

"And what about his trade? I had no idea he'd turn out to be a blacksmith."

"Hmm. His trade. Well, he had the muscles built up in all the right places to be a blacksmith, and some soot permanently ground in behind his right ear where I suspect he rubs his hand when he's vexed. You'll pick up on it quick enough after you've talked to a few newcomers."

Jacob paced across the floor. "I don't know, Uncle Will. Maybe I'm not cut out for this."

"Why? What's the matter? You're not quittin' before you even give it a chance, eh?"

"What are you going to say to this Knight fellow when you get back to Riverton and he wants to know why you didn't tell him the truth—that there's no town, not a horse within two miles that'll need

101

shoeing, and all that fertile farmland is beneath a dense forest?"

Will waved his concern aside. "Jacob, by the time Isaac Knight and I meet again, he'll have resigned himself to his circumstances. The others will tell him Riverton's a fine settlement to live in, but it'll take some work. Besides, he doesn't have the cash to move elsewhere. He spent most of what he had on Riverton." Will rested his elbows on his knees. "Now, why don't you go on over to your room and send my wife along. See you in the morning at breakfast."

CHAPTER 8

"I TOLD YOU THE FIRST DAY, Elizabeth, that you should take advantage of the opportunity and shop. Tomorrow, we go home, and what have you bought for yourself? What has Jacob bought for you? Nothing," Louisa admonished. It was late afternoon, and the women took tea in the ladies' parlor while their husbands tended to business.

"Guess I just didn't see anything that caught my eye, and Jacob's been too busy. You know he and Will have been gone every day, selling land, or checking with the engravers."

These were just excuses. In truth, she had seen a few things she would have liked to buy, but wanted Jacob's opinion on them first. She was disappointed that he hadn't yet had time to go with her to look at them, but realized it might have been on purpose. Though he hadn't come right out and said so, she thought he was glad she hadn't spent the money he had given her for shopping. At least, he had been asking her about it at the end of each day. His concern made her feel uneasy about spending their hard cash money right now. Besides, she felt nervous about Jacob and Will having the notes printed so they could establish their bank once they returned to Riverton. Keeping some hard cash money aside seemed like a good precaution.

Louisa set down her tea cup and leaned forward. "I've been so caught up with shopping, I forgot to mention, Will says we'll have new neighbors when we get back to Riverton! A blacksmith bought some land for his family and they've already gone up on the *Governor Marcy*."

Elizabeth had only been half listening. "That's nice, I hope they like it there." Then, with a sudden spark of interest, she added, "Did you say a black-smith?"

"Yes, a smith with four young 'uns, Will told me."

"That's a coincidence. My Aunt Sallie told me her husband is a blacksmith."

"Maybe he's the one Will sold the land to," Louisa conjectured. "That'd be real nice for you, having your relatives nearby again."

Elizabeth thought for a moment. She had told Jacob about seeing her Aunt Sallie, and how her husband was a blacksmith looking for land, but Jacob hadn't mentioned the coincidence, and in fact had barely been listening to her. "No, they couldn't have been the ones Will sold to," she concluded. "Aunt Sallie specifically said her husband was going to buy prairie land."

Louisa shrugged. "Well, whoever it is, I hope we'll like our new neighbors, and they'll like us. I always look forward to newcomers."

Will and Jacob had inspected their freshly printed notes for the Riverton Bank in the print shop. Now, they took them to Will's room to look them over again.

Will held up two notes as he rubbed them between

his fingers. "Just think of it, Jacob, thousands of dollars' worth of notes. With all that paper money circulatin' about, Riverton's gonna boom!"

"I sure hope you're right, and that the merchants in Upper Saginaw take to the new currency." Jacob sat, slumped on the room's only chair.

"Take to it? They'll be scrappin' for it. Especially since I told 'em I'd put the bank right on the Riverton-Upper Saginaw line so it would be real convenient, seein' that the Upper Saginaw folk didn't take the initiative to start their own bank. Don't you worry, my boy, long as Pierce's are invested, they'll accept our notes at their store in trade for goods. Since theirs is the biggest business in that town, the rest of the shop owners will fall right in line."

"I sure hope you're right about the bank, and it's a big success. I can't afford trips like this one, if my land doesn't sell faster than it did this week." Jacob loosened his cravat.

"I'm sure sorry you didn't sell any of that section you bought from me. Of course, I would've liked to have sold more myself." Will fastened the leather straps around the satchel containing the bank notes and set it aside, then sat on the bed. "At least I sold forty acres to that Knight fellow. It made the whole trip worthwhile, the price he paid."

Jacob looked away from his grinning uncle's face to the toes of his boots, realizing subconsciously he had had a hard time meeting people eye to eye this past week. "I kind of wonder about Isaac Knight and his family sometimes. It took most of his money to buy land at that price."

"Who's to worry? I saw what he had left, and there was enough to buy supplies that'll see him and his family through the winter. Besides, no one starves up in Riverton, not with those Indians always eager to trade a three-foot-long troutpike for a bottle of cheap whiskey. And Pierce's will carry you for a good long while before they cut off your credit." Will stood and sauntered toward the door. "Well, I'm going down to the tap room to celebrate. Care to join me?"

Jacob shook his head, and followed his uncle out the door. "Guess I'll take a rest before supper."

Alone in his room, Jacob lay on the bed thinking about his uncle's way of doing business. Jacob knew in his own mind one of the reasons he hadn't been able to sell any land was because he couldn't operate like his uncle did, misrepresenting forest as prairie—or whatever the potential buyer was looking for. He still felt guilty over the Knight sale. Sure, Will had done the talking, and taken the man's money, but Jacob had helped him do it by not speaking the truth.

All his uncle's enthusiasm about the bank troubled him, too. He knew that only half of the value of the notes they had had printed was backed by hard cash money. All the remaining assets were tied up in land, and some of it was overvalued to his way of thinking. They might pass inspection when the bank inspector showed up to verify their deposits of silver and gold, but talk was some new banks were about to fail, and if they did, word would soon spread, and they would drag other banks down with them. From his years in the banking business with his father, the one ingredient Jacob knew was essential to success was customer confidence. Once customers got nervous, failure was just around the corner.

It was hard cash, not bank notes that had become valuable lately. He had heard talk this week about some who were hoarding what little hard cash they had. President Jackson acknowledged that problem when he issued the specie circular last year, requiring payment in hard cash money for public lands. Even Jacob felt compelled to hang onto what hard cash he had left. Most of his was gone now, invested into the bank. Of course, as soon as the bank opened he would have to take a mortgage out on his unfinished house and extra land parcels.

Since Jacob's cash reserves from the endowment had dwindled considerably, he was glad Elizabeth hadn't spent the coins he had given her. He had asked her every night after she had been with Louisa shopping all day long whether she had spent any money, and every day so far, she had said no. Had she suspected he was worried about money, and purposely not spent any? He felt bad now that he had not shopped once with her the whole week they had been there, but they might need the money they had left, to tide them over until the bank got on its feet, and he sold some of that land.

He felt bad that he had misled her about selling his land, too. She had asked him each day how it was going, and he had told her not to worry, business was fine, that he had been meeting people every day who were interested in buying land. He had avoided saying he had not sold any land, but he was going to have to do just that very soon to keep solvent. He would *have* to!

Yes, by golly, I will *sell that land*, Jacob resolved to himself. *And once I do, Elizabeth will see I was right about this business.*

The door opened, and Jacob looked up to see Elizabeth enter the room. The first thing he noticed about her was the absence of packages. He took a deep, relieved breath.

"Jacob, I didn't know you were back. I just came to wash up and get ready for supper." Elizabeth deposited her little drawstring bag on the table and moved to the pitcher and washbasin.

Jacob got up off the bed and sat in a chair. "How was your day? Did you and Louisa have a good time?" He waited until her back was to him, then lifted the purse, testing its weight, reassuring himself that the cash was still inside.

"It was all right, I suppose, But I'm ready to go back to Riverton, after all the hustle and bustle of

Detroit." Elizabeth splashed her face with water, then dried herself with a towel. "Say, Louisa told me we're getting new neighbors." She hung the towel over its bar and turned to look at Jacob. "Is something troubling you? You look worried."

"I'm fine, really," he assured his wife as he moved from the chair to lie across the soft bed again.

Elizabeth sat on the edge of the bed and took his hand. "Louisa told me Will sold some land to a blacksmith. Why didn't you mention it?"

"Guess it slipped my mind," he hedged, wishing the topic hadn't come up to remind him of his involvement, if only tacit, in the deal.

"Did you meet the people? What were they like?"

"I met the fellow, then after Will closed the deal, he and I helped the man and his wife and four children on the *Governor Marcy*. You'll meet them when you get home. Their name is Knight. They seem like good, honest, hard-working people."

"Four children, you said?" Elizabeth looked puzzled. "What an odd coincidence. Remember my telling you the other day about seeing my Aunt Sallie?"

Jacob's brows came together, then he shook his head. "I guess I don't. Was she the aunt who took care of you for so many years, the one you were so fond of?"

"Yes, she's the one. Well, she and her husband have four children, and he's a blacksmith. She never did tell me her married name, but it couldn't have been Knight." Elizabeth shook her head slowly from side to side. "They couldn't be the ones Will sold his land to. Her husband was buying land from somebody, but she told me he was after prairie land. She said she couldn't possibly stand to live in the forest like we do. Much as I'd want her for a neighbor, we both knew they'd be terribly unhappy in Riverton, after I described it to her, and there's nothing worse than an unhappy neighbor, Papa used to say."

Jacob's heart sank. "Elizabeth," he propped himself up on an elbow, "I'm fairly certain it *was* your Aunt Sallie's husband who bought the forty acres from Will."

"No," she shook her head, "it doesn't make sense. Why would he buy in Riverton when he wanted prairie land?"

Jacob got up and paced toward the door, wondering how to answer. "I guess . . . he must have thought it was prairie when he bought it," he mentioned hesitantly.

"But whatever gave him that impression?"

Jacob's stomach turned sour as he thought about the reason.

"Jacob, please answer me! Why did Aunt Sallie's husband think he was buying prairie?"

"Certainly not because of anything I said," Jacob defended himself.

"Will. It was Will, wasn't it?" She demanded, then without waiting for his answer, continued. "Will duped him with his stories and his map of the town, didn't he?" She clenched her hands into fists, then unclenched them. "Well, didn't he?" she repeated louder.

"Elizabeth, calm down." Jacob's voice was smooth.

"Calm down?" she asked, her tone rising with anger. "How could you let him do that to my relatives?"

"I didn't know they were your relatives," Jacob quickly reminded her.

"Relatives or not, how could you let Will do it at all? You were there when he sold the land. Why didn't you speak up and tell the truth about it?" She swung open the door.

"Elizabeth—" Jacob called. But she was gone.

Elizabeth's anger engulfed her as she flew down the hall to Will and Louisa's room. She knew from the footsteps behind her that Jacob was following, but nothing could stop her from confronting her husband's uncle. She pounded on the door, turning the doorknob at the same time. The door was locked.

"Will, Louisa," she called, pounding furiously. "Let me in!"

She heard shuffling and muffled voices from inside.

Jacob stood behind her. "Shh, Elizabeth, calm down and listen to me," he urged her.

"I've heard enough from you, Jacob." She pounded on the door again. Suddenly, it opened, and she stepped past Will inside. Jacob followed her in and closed the door as quickly as possible.

"Will Morgan, I hate you! I hate what you do, and what Jacob is doing because of you. How could you do it? How could you cheat my relatives?" She paced to the end of the room and turned abruptly, taking a split second to notice Will's and Louisa's stunned faces.

Recovering from his initial shock, Will let a slow grin creep over his features. "Well, well now, Elizabeth, calm down. What's this talk about cheatin' your relatives? I don't understand."

"Don't play innocent with me, Will Morgan, you understand perfectly well what I'm talking about, selling forest land for prairie, telling a blacksmith there's a town up at Riverton when there's a half dozen log cabins. How many other people did you lie to this week just to sell them some of your forest?"

Will chuckled. "What the devil are you so upset about? *You* thought there was a town there when you came, but you stayed on in spite of the truth. Your relatives will, too, and they'll be glad they did. That land's gonna be worth a fortune one of these days, then we'll all be a whole lot richer than we are right now."

"Rich! Is that all you can think about, getting rich by taking advantage of people? Obviously you value your own personal gain over honesty. Once, I was willing to forgive you for it, but not any more!" She stormed out of the room, and down the hall.

When she reached her own room, Elizabeth quickly locked the door behind her, then threw herself on the bed and cried.

Jacob knocked on the door. "Elizabeth?" He called quietly, then knocked some more. "Elizabeth, let me in."

"I want to be alone," she told him, through stifled sobs.

"Elizabeth unlock the door," Jacob said sternly.

"Go away," she murmured, then wept bitterly.

For a long time, she continued crying, soaking her handkerchiefs, one after another until all that she had brought with her on the trip were thoroughly wet. How could she ever face her aunt after what had happened? She felt deep shame and embarrassment. Aunt Sallie, whom she'd loved nearly as much as her own mother, would be crushed to learn that her niece's husband had been part of a dishonest scheme. To think Will had told Sallie's husband he was buying prairie land was too much!

When she had recovered from the initial shock of what had happened, her thoughts turned to Jacob's part in it. She had always considered Jacob a deeply honest man. Had she been wrong about him?

How could he fail to speak out when Will intentionally misled people for the purpose of making money?

"Jacob, Jacob, how could you do it?" she murmured to herself. "I thought I knew you. I loved the man I thought you were, but now . . ."

Could she really stop loving him? She knew he was a good man—she *knew* it—but he had made a huge mistake, an unforgivable mistake that would damage more than one relationship. Yet, the longer she dwelt on the impossibility of forgiving him, the stronger came the unbidden memory of Mae Clarke's words. "Everyone needs room to make mistakes, and when we do, that's when we need forgiveness more than ever."

Elizabeth mulled the thought over in her mind for a while. Certainly she would want Jacob to forgive her when she made mistakes. Gradually, it came to her that the most troubling aspect of the whole concept was that she feared Jacob might never recognize his action as being a mistake.

"Maybe he's like Will and I didn't realize it," she muttered, then added, "no, he isn't, he *can't* be!" She tried to reassure herself, but the more she thought about it, the more confused and frustrated she became, until her mind was a jumble of thoughts and emotions swirling and swirling, lulling her into a half sleep.

Finally, she whispered into the darkness, "Please, Lord, help me through this." She closed her eyes, and exhaustion overtook her.

Hours later, in pitch darkness, Elizabeth reached across the bed to the empty place where Jacob usually lay. Then, the horrid realization came flooding back, the memories of her confrontation with Will and her anger at Jacob, and the fact that she had left Jacob locked out of the room. She got up and unlocked the door. There, slumped in the hallway, was Jacob. He stirred the moment he realized she had opened the door, reaching out for her.

She stepped inside the room, avoiding his touch, and slipped between the sheets again. Jacob came into the room, dropped his boots on the floor, and undressed, then slid under the covers. She kept her back to him. He leaned over her, and caressed her cheek with the back of his hand.

"I'm sorry, Elizabeth," he whispered, "I never meant to hurt you."

She turned toward him. "You're sorry only because you hurt me? What about the Knights? Don't you realize how wrong you were, how wrong Will was?"

"I won't answer for another man's actions. I never wanted you to feel hurt. I love you. Let's get some sleep." Turning his back to her, he laid on his side.

Elizabeth lay awake for a while, thinking. She knew Jacob loved her, as she loved him, and along with his apology, she wondered if she could justify her continued anger. Still, he couldn't wipe away the damage with his two simple phrases, "I'm sorry, Elizabeth . . . I never meant to hurt you." She wished the whole incident had been a nightmare from which she could awaken, but it wasn't. She lapsed into a troubled, fitful sleep.

The following morning, Jacob and Elizabeth barely spoke to one another as they prepared to board the steamer for Riverton. It wasn't just Jacob whom Elizabeth had no desire to speak with—she didn't care to talk with anybody—not Louisa, and especially not Uncle Will.

Once on board, she stood at the rail, letting the breeze buffet her face for a long time as she sorted out what she would say to Aunt Sallie when she saw her. With sadness, Elizabeth realized that words would never be sufficient.

Later, Jacob joined her at the rail. "Elizabeth, I know you're still very upset—"

"Upset doesn't begin to describe how I feel, Jacob," she interrupted, surprising even herself with the terseness in her voice. "I feel completely betrayed by both you and Uncle Will." She turned away, keeping her eyes on the water.

"I'm sorry, Elizabeth. Can't you accept my apology?"

"It's a little late for being sorry. The damage is done, and the wrong can't be righted." She turned to face him. "Not even if Uncle Will gave Aunt Sallie's husband all his money back, which I know he'd never do, as greedy as he is."

Jacob grasped her shoulders firmly. "Elizabeth, I love you. Do you hear me? I love you, and would never, for all the world, hurt you on purpose. Please forgive me for any part I had in it, and let's go on from there."

"I forgive you," she said unconvincingly, "but as long as you're involved in these dealings with Uncle Will, you'll never have my respect. Being a party to his way of doing business is inexcusable." She turned to walk away.

He caught her by the elbow and swung her around. "Then I'll tell him I want out. Just as soon as I can, I'll be free of my agreements with him."

She looked into his blue eyes, searching for a shred of sincerity. "And what did it cost you to make *that* promise, Jacob Morgan? Very little, I would guess, as I suspect you're already up to your eyeballs in dealings with him."

This time, when she walked away, Jacob didn't try to stop her. She wished he had, wished he would tell her he had not buried himself in commitments to his uncle. But he let her go, and she knew then she had guessed accurately.

As the steamer entered the mouth of the Saginaw River that afternoon, Louisa knocked at Elizabeth's door and entered quietly. They hadn't spoken to one another since Elizabeth had unleashed her anger at Will the night before.

"Elizabeth," she began hesitantly, "I know you're still upset with Will, and I'm not sure as I blame ya', but I wanted you to know he's gonna give your aunt and her family the use of our cabin till their own is ready. That way, they won't have to stay in a hut while they're buildin' on their own land."

"It's kind of you to offer, Louisa, but with the three of you and Sallie's family of six, it just wouldn't work. Your cabin is too small."

Louisa shook her head. "Oh, but you're wrong. Will, Jeremy, and I won't be livin' there. We're moving into the loft of the blockhouse before tonight. Will fixed it all up for us, special," she explained. "I'll talk to your aunt about it as soon as we get to Riverton, if it's all right with you."

"Fine, Louisa, and thank you." Elizabeth tried to smile, but she knew her effort fell short.

When Elizabeth had disembarked at Riverton, she sought out Sallie and Isaac's building site. She stood on the riverbank alone for a few moments, sizing up their piece of land. It was a prime site. At least she would give Will credit for that. It had a sloping bank to the water, steep enough to retain spring floods, but gentle enough for easy access to the river from shore. She could hear an ax working back in from the shoreline, and headed toward the sound.

When she approached the opening, she saw that Isaac and his oldest son each toiled with an ax, hacking up the trunk of a felled tree, while Sallie and the younger boy cleared away the debris and heaped it in a pile to be burned once the wood had dried sufficiently. On the edge of the clearing stood a temporary hovel they had built, one side open, the top covered with cedar boughs.

Sallie looked up as Elizabeth entered the clearing, then immediately resumed her task, ignoring her. Elizabeth slowly approached, wondering what words she could say that wouldn't sound trite and insufficient. At last, she stood within a few feet of her aunt.

"Aunt Sallie?" She waited, but her aunt continued to ignore her. "Aunt Sallie, I'm sorry the way things turned out for you. . . ."

Sallie bent over, adding more branches to her

armload, then turned to face her. Perspiration beaded on her brow. "Elizabeth, I'm too disappointed right now to speak with a civil tongue, and I'm asking you to leave, before I say something to you I'll regret."

"I just want you to know I had no idea—"

Sallie interrupted. "I know you'd never wish ill on me and my family, but what's done is done. Now please go."

Elizabeth hesitated. Behind her, she heard branches crackling underfoot. Someone entered the clearing. Her eyes strayed to Isaac. He lifted his rifle and fired a warning shot, blasting a branch off a nearby tree. She turned around to see Jacob dodging the falling limb.

Isaac shouted, "Hold it right there, you scoundrel, or your next step will be your last."

CHAPTER 9

"DON'T DO SOMETHING YOU'LL REGRET. Isaac," Jacob
warned, then he spoke to his wife. "Come on,
Elizabeth. We're not welcome here. Let's go."

Reluctantly, Elizabeth turned away, realizing this
was not the time to heal so fresh a wound. In silence,
she and Jacob walked along the riverbank. Their own
plot of land lay between the main settlement and the
Knight's land, and Jacob took her hand as they
approached it. "Come on. Take a look at our house.
It's been a while since you've seen it, and the
carpenters made a lot of progress the week before we
went to Detroit. Besides, you haven't seen the
stonemason's work yet."

Elizabeth pulled her hand away. "Don't try to
assuage my anger with talk of how the house is
coming."

Jacob stepped in front of her. "Don't do this,
Elizabeth. Don't drive a wedge between us," he
pleaded.

"Then change the way things are, Jacob." Her
watery eyes met his. "Promise me you're not like

117

Will, that you'll never be a part of a deal like the one he made with Isaac Knight, and *keep* your promise." As she blinked, tears trickled down her cheeks.

Jacob wrapped his arms around her so tightly, she couldn't breathe for a moment. "I give you my word, Elizabeth, and I'll make good on it." He kissed her hair.

The security of Jacob's embrace once again made Elizabeth want to believe his promises, but tiny doubts remained stubbornly lodged in the corner of her mind.

A few moments later, she released herself from his arms. Jacob followed her as she stepped into the clearing where their new house was being built.

Her eyes rested on the two-story frame house with clapboard siding all around, a wide front door, and six-pane windows on either side. It stood taller and more imposing than she had remembered. Though the upper floor was not as far along as the lower, six-pane windows had already been installed there also.

As Elizabeth looked at the home she and Jacob had talked about only months before, her emotions were a mixture of sadness and joy. She felt bad that she harbored doubts about her husband's integrity, and guilty that her aunt's family had been living steps away in a hovel. At the same time, she felt excited to be entering her new home.

Jacob opened the massive front door for her to enter. "Soon, the first floor will be completed and we can move in. I'd say in three weeks' time, it'll be far enough along."

"Three weeks?" Elizabeth asked with surprise as she stepped inside onto wide pine board flooring. "Jacob," she turned to face her husband, "I know you wanted all new furniture for the house, but I've sensed you're a little short on cash. Is it all right if I write Papa and ask him to ship the used furniture?"

Jacob nodded reluctantly. Taking her hands in his,

he said, "Elizabeth, I'd like you to give me all the hard cash money you had left from the trip so I can put it in safe keeping. I'll give you some bank notes to use at the general store. You can place an order with Mrs. Pierce for any special needs you might have for the house, like curtains."

Elizabeth nodded, then turned and walked into the common room, and on into the kitchen. When Elizabeth saw the beehive oven and wide kitchen fireplace with an ample hearth, her enthusiasm mounted. "Oh, Jacob, I can hardly believe it. With an oven like this, I'll be able to bake bread, and cakes, and pies . . ."

Jacob grinned and pulled her close, then a solemn expression overtook his features. "Elizabeth, I love you so very much. I want only the best for us." He captured her face in his hands and pressed a firm kiss against her lips. "Do you believe me?"

Elizabeth searched Jacob's serious blue eyes as she traced his cheekbone with her finger. "Of course I believe you love me, Jacob, but maybe you want the best a little too much," she suggested.

A moment later, they heard someone's "ehhemm," and looked up to find Louisa standing in the doorway. "Didn't mean to interrupt you folks, but I need to talk with ya'."

Elizabeth stepped away from Jacob and beckoned her inside. "What is it, Louisa?"

"I've just been to see the Knights." She moved her head slowly from side to side. "They aren't takin' to Riverton at all."

Jacob nodded. "So we found out. We've just come from their lot. Seems they weren't in the mood for talking."

Louisa rolled her eyes. "You'd think I insulted them by offerin' them my cabin, the way Mr. Knight took to his gun an' invited me to get off his property." She shook her head. "That hut o' theirs isn't much.

I'm sure the little ones are sleepin' under the stars. They'd all be so much more comfortable in a cabin, an' I think Mrs. Knight was ready to accept the offer, but that husband o' hers got all cussed and told me they don't want charity.''

Elizabeth looked to Jacob for an answer. "You did all you could, Louisa. Isaac Knight will learn in time that in a pioneer settlement, neighbors depend on each other. The weather's dry right now, but I suspect a little rain will hasten their move into your place.''

Louisa tilted one corner of her mouth upward. "I believe you're right 'bout that, Jacob. I'll just wait until the weather's right to make my offer again.''

After she had left, Jacob took Elizabeth's hand. "Offering that cabin to the Knights was all Louisa's idea. Will was going to try to sell it and the land that goes with it when we were in Detroit, but the only land he sold was to the Knights. When Louisa discovered what had happened with your relatives, she suggested to Will that the Knights could use their cabin. He wondered why he hadn't thought of it himself.''

Elizabeth felt her anger rising. "Isn't that just like Will. Louisa didn't have much when she was a widow, but at least that cabin and land were her own. Now that she's married, what little she *did* own belongs to Will, and leave it to him to try and profit from it,'' she fumed. As she paced across the floor, she wondered if her anger at Will would ever decrease in intensity.

"Calm down, Elizabeth. I know you don't think much of Will right now, but he *did* help keep Louisa going when she was newly widowed, and he really does love her. He only does what he thinks is best.''

"Why does 'what's best' always have a price tag on it where Will's concerned?''

"Maybe someday you can persuade him to think otherwise.''

"I doubt either one of us will live long enough for that to happen."

The next two days provided warm September weather with sunny days, and chilly nights. "Perfect for building a bank," Jacob had said. He left early each morning with Will, returning after dark. Elizabeth still felt a reserve toward her husband, one she thought would last as long as Jacob's business dealings were tied to Will Morgan.

Because Jacob had said their house would be ready within three weeks, Elizabeth penned a letter to her father. She had written him only one other time, and then only a short note to assure him of her safe arrival. Now, she asked him to ship her the furniture he had offered them.

She wrote:

> I hope that the items will reach Riverton before the shipping lanes close for the season. Otherwise, our spacious new home will look empty throughout the winter. It is similar in size to your home in Stockport, with extra bedrooms upstairs and a large common room on the first floor, so you can imagine how barren the unfurnished rooms can be.

In her letter, she also mentioned how she had crossed paths with Aunt Sallie, and that her family had become the newest Riverton residents, though she avoided mention of the strife between Isaac Knight and others in the community. She had never told her father that the town she thought existed before coming to Riverton had yet to be built.

> As you can tell, Riverton is growing. Sallie's husband is a blacksmith by trade, and Jacob's uncle will soon open a bank. We already have a reverend, and several residents depend upon farming for a living. No doctor has yet come here to live, so I am thankful to have the small supply of medicines on hand that you sent with me. I have not had to call upon them since administering the smallpox vaccine in July.

Since I last wrote you, I have learned that Jacob and I will become parents in April. If we lived closer, you could have the privilege of delivering your first grandchild! Since hundreds of miles separate us, and there are no medical doctors nearby, I expect a midwife will attend the delivery, and I will inquire soon into who might be available for the task.

We send our love to you, and hope you are well.

Affectionately, Elizabeth and Jacob.

The month was drawing to a close. Still troubled over her reception by her aunt, and angry with Uncle Will, Elizabeth remained in her cabin most of the time. She hadn't seen Mae Clarke during her first two days back from Detroit, but neither had she been in a good humor for visiting. On the third morning after her return, a knock came at her door, and she knew before she opened it Mrs. Clarke would be standing on the other side.

"Are you feeling all right, Elizabeth? I've been worried about you," her kind neighbor asked.

"I'm fine, thank you, Mrs. Clarke."

Mrs. Clarke looked at her skeptically. "You're sure?"

Elizabeth wondered if her unhappiness was still evident in her expression, and made an effort to give a genuine smile. "Positive. Would you like to come in for some tea?"

"I don't want to interrupt anything."

All at once, Elizabeth realized how much she would enjoy a talk with her understanding neighbor. "Nothing that couldn't improve with some interrupting. A chat with you is just what I need to brighten my outlook."

The tea steeped while Elizabeth recounted her experiences in Detroit; meeting her beloved Aunt Sallie, then learning later about the sale of the land.

"I suppose I'm still angry with Jacob for his part in it," she concluded, "I think he realizes how wrong he

122

was, and how much he's hurt me, but I'm not sure it will change things."

"You can't go on being upset with your husband forever, Elizabeth. If he's apologized, then you need to put anger behind you."

Elizabeth thought for a moment. "I know you're right. I think I just need a little more time. If there's anything good to be said about it, it's that my disappointment in Jacob is mild compared to my anger at Uncle Will. He came between my aunt and me before we had a chance to get to know each other again. I'm not sure I'll ever forgive him for that, at least not until he's changed his ways, and stopped misleading people."

Mrs. Clarke's expression looked troubled. "I understand what you're saying. Perhaps, with prayer, you can find a way to help Will deal honestly with others, and you can forgive him."

Elizabeth looked down. "I know you're right, but . . ."

"Elizabeth, look at me," Mrs. Clarke entreated. "I'd like to tell you something about Riverton that I'm certain no one has explained to you. It will help you understand Will Morgan, and might ease your mind until emotions settle down a little between you and the Knights." She sipped the last of her tea and set her cup aside. "When Will Morgan came here, there was nothing but forest and Indians. He saw something in this location—the bend in the river, the tall pines growing up out of rich, black soil—that he thought someday would amount to something. Once the government survey was done and the land went up for sale, he bought it on auction. Ever since then, he's worked his heart out to make a decent village out of this clearing in the forest.

"There's not a settler among us who wasn't duped to some degree by Will's description of his land, to be sure. The Knights might be a little angrier than most, but we all fell for a story of sorts, be it about a town that didn't have streets yet, or a prairie that's not to be found. Now, I'm not saying I agree with his methods, but once a man buys land from Will Morgan, he's gained himself a loyal supporter. Will's helped every one of us adjust to this life. He's worked hard as an ox to help us raise our cabins, and tided us over in winter when food was scarce by trading with the Indians for their extra corn. You see, Will Morgan has a dream to make Riverton into a thriving city one day, and he knows if people leave just because times get tough out here, he'll never see his dream come true. That's why it means so much to him to draw people up here. A town couldn't have a more ambitious promoter."

"But the way he does it—"

"Like I said, I don't agree with his methods. I'm just trying to tell you about a side of him you've never seen before, a good side. The Knights are pretty upset right now because they feel wronged, and they feel trapped, but you give Will Morgan a little time, and I'll bet you he'll have a house raising organized with enough men from Upper Saginaw combined with our own Riverton fellows to set them up with a cabin in a day or two." Mrs. Clarke's earnest expression melted into a smile. "Clara Langton will be around the moment she gets wind of it to organize the cooking. You can be sure of that."

The corners of Elizabeth's mouth turned upward. "I was kind of puzzled over why she and everyone else made such a fuss over Will's wedding. I guess now I know."

"We've all come to respect him, after a fashion, Elizabeth. He's been there when we've needed him. But you have to be willing to look past that other side of him."

Puzzling thoughts ran through her mind, and she realized too late, she had been scowling.

"Something must still be troubling you, Elizabeth," Mrs. Clarke observed. "What is it?"

"Mrs. Clarke, if Will's so set on making Riverton into a special place to live, why hasn't he even built himself a frame house?"

"That exact question crossed my mind, though I've never put it to Will. You know what I've concluded?"

Elizabeth shook her head.

"Will Morgan's been too busy seeing to everyone else's needs to worry about a frame house for himself. A man can survive in just about anything for a shelter, but a woman needs a home. I suspect now that he's married, he'll be doing something about building one for Louisa."

One day later, on the first day of October, the fall storms began. Early that morning, loud claps of thunder and ominous rumblings woke Elizabeth before the first light of dawn.

There was still an underlying current of tension between her and Jacob, a certain reserve that was almost tangible at times, but in many aspects, their relationship appeared normal. She leaned over him after a particularly loud crack of thunder. "Jacob? You awake?"

"With that racket going on outside, I couldn't sleep," he mumbled.

"Me either." She laid back against her pillow and listened to the raindrops begin to fall.

"Your aunt and her husband will get soaked." Jacob voiced her own concern. "I'd better go see about moving them and their belongings into Louisa's cabin." He arose and started dressing.

"I'll come, too." Elizabeth swung her feet to the floor.

"No. I don't want you out in this weather." Jacob put a restraining hand on her shoulder. "You have more to think about than just yourself, you know." He looked at her thickening waistline.

"I'll make breakfast, then. It will be ready when you get back," she promised, "and don't come home alone. I'll prepare enough griddle cakes for the Knights, too."

Jacob looked doubtful. "I wouldn't count on their eating at our table," he cautioned her. "No telling what I'll run into when I get to their place." He pulled on his jacket and cap, and set out in the now pouring rain.

Elizabeth rekindled her fire then mixed a triple batch of pancake batter. Her cooking had improved considerably since her arrival at Riverton. She fried panful after panful of griddle cakes, removing them to a warm covered pan to the side of the fire after they'd become golden brown. When she finished, she opened the cabin door to look for any sign of Jacob or the Knights, but no one was in sight.

She worried that something dreadful might have happened, and remembered the rifle Isaac seemed ready to point in the direction of trespassers. Would he actually be angry enough to use it against Jacob? Against someone who had come to help him?

As she paced the cabin floor, her apprehension overcame her. She couldn't bear the thought that Jacob's life might be in danger, that he might become the victim of Isaac's wrath. "I *do* love him, I *really do* love him," she admitted, with an ache in her heart.

She reached for her cloak and dashed out into the downpour, running as much of the way as she could, then slowing to a brisk walk toward the Knight's cabin site. With each flash of lightning and crack of thunder, icy raindrops fell harder and faster, stinging her face.

Rain soaked through her woolen cloak sending cold chills up her spine. With every step, mud splashed on her skirt, and oozed over the tops of her shoes; dampness seeped through the seams around the soles. As she neared the Knight's land, she heard men shouting. She stepped into the clearing to find the sides clearly drawn: Isaac stood with his two sons next to the leaky hut, while Sallie and her daughters huddled inside. A stack of belongings—chests, barrels, and leather bags—stood in a puddle next to the hovel. Isaac's gun held dead aim at Will; Jacob stood only a few paces away.

Isaac shouted over the rumbling thunder, "I warned you 'bout coming near me. Now git on home, 'fore I fix ya' so ya' can't."

Will answered him boldly. "Don't be foolhardy, Isaac Knight. Think of your wife and daughters, shiverin' beneath that leaky pile of branches. At least let them come to the cabin where they can warm up and dry off." Will took a step forward.

Isaac pointed his rifle to the sky and let off a warning shot. "Don't come no closer now, you thief."

Jacob stepped beside his uncle. "Your supplies will be ruined if you don't get them out of the rain soon. You'll have nothin' but flour paste in that barrel, then what will you eat this winter? Be reasonable, Knight, let us move them into the blockhouse."

Sallie pleaded with her husband. "Listen to reason, Isaac. We can't take the chance of losing what little we've got. You know we've got to make it through the winter with those supplies."

Isaac turned to look at his wife. "Hush up, Sallie. I'll handle this."

While he was talking to her, Will moved ahead another pace.

Todd shouted, "Pa, watch out!"

Isaac swung around and let off an indiscriminate shot. Will ducked, and lunged at him simultaneously, landing on top of him in the mud. He wrested Isaac's rifle from him and flung it out of reach.

Todd and Charles jumped on Will. Jacob scrambled to pull them off.

"Boys, no!" Sallie yelled, running from the hut.

Mayhem ensued. Arms and legs flew wildly as mud splashed in the air. Shouts and groans erupted. When the mess untangled, Sallie and Jacob each held a boy by the back of his collar, while Will restrained Isaac, pinning his arms against the ground.

"Now," Will said to Isaac, "we're gonna save you a lot of hungry nights this winter. Either you can help us, or you can stay out here in the rain and catch a lousy cold, 'cause I'm gonna tie you to a tree if you'd rather not cooperate. Now which will it be?"

Todd shouted, "Don't give in, Pa!" He jabbed his elbows into Jacob's ribs. "Let me go!"

Jacob held the boy firmly.

"Calm down, Todd," Sallie admonished sternly. She turned to Isaac. "I've got to take the girls where it's warm and dry." She released Charles's collar.

Amy and Sarah ran to her side.

Elizabeth joined them. "I'll take you to Louisa's cabin," she offered, shivering so hard she could barely speak.

Sallie nodded.

Will released Isaac, then called to Elizabeth. "Louisa's already got a fire goin' at the cabin. Tell her I'll be ready for a hearty meal soon as I finish moving these goods into the blockhouse."

Elizabeth nodded, but didn't reply. She couldn't help but think that her relatives would never have found themselves in such a wretched situation if he hadn't lied to them in the first place.

CHAPTER 10

AMY AND SARAH clung to their mother as they followed Elizabeth up the trail toward Louisa's cabin. No words were spoken. As they approached the cluster of cabins in the village settlement, Sarah slipped in the mud, and Elizabeth instinctively reached out to help her. The child pulled away from Elizabeth's touch as if she had been burned, and scrambled to her feet. It was then that Elizabeth realized how completely resentment had pervaded her aunt's family.

Elizabeth was thankful to reach Louisa's cabin door and pull the latch string. When they entered, Louisa hurried from the fire to greet them.

"Goodness, you're soaked to the bone. Let me help you out of those wet things. Amy, would you like some help?" She stooped to take the girl's cloak.

"No!" Amy pulled back and reached for her mother.

Sallie put her arm around Amy then spoke to Louisa almost coldly. "Please leave us alone here for a while."

Louisa gave Sallie a puzzled look, as if she hadn't heard correctly. "I've got hot herb tea steeping, and eggs ready to go into the pan. You look as though you could do with a good hot breakfast."

"No need. Please just go. You said we'd be welcome to use your cabin. I thank you for your generous offer. Now, if you could let us be." Sallie unhooked her own cloak and hung it on a peg.

Elizabeth spoke to her aunt. "I've got a panful of flapjacks keeping warm by my fire for you. I'll go get them."

Sallie shook her head. "Don't go to the trouble."

"No trouble," she commented as she stepped out into the rain once more.

When she returned to Louisa's cabin, Sallie and her daughters were warming themselves by the fire, and Louisa was pulling on her cloak. Elizabeth set the pan of cakes down near the fire and said to her aunt. "My cabin's directly across the way if you need anything."

Sallie nodded. "Thank you. Goodbye." Her tone remained icy.

When the door had closed behind Elizabeth and Louisa, Elizabeth spoke. "Will said to tell you he'd be ready for a hearty meal once he's moved the Knights' goods into the blockhouse."

"I'd best be tendin' to my fire then." Louisa looked back at the cabin she had once occupied and added, "Sure is a sour bunch in there."

"You missed all the excitement over at the Knights' parcel. Isaac held Will and Jacob at gunpoint until Will knocked him onto his back in the mud. If it weren't for the rain, I doubt Aunt Sallie would have spoken to us yet."

"I suppose you're right, the way that family's feelin' about Riverton." When they reached the point where the path split in two, one going toward the blockhouse and the other toward Elizabeth's cabin, Louisa asked, "Why don't you and Jacob eat breakfast with us?"

Elizabeth shook her head. "Thanks for the invitation, but I made plenty of flapjacks. I'll just wait for Jacob to come home." She didn't admit her real reason for refusing—not wanting to spend any time at all near Will. She had no desire to hurt Louisa's feelings further.

"I'll see you some other time then. Stop up to the blockhouse, Elizabeth. We've got a cozy place fixed up in the loft. I want to show it to you."

"Thanks for the invitation," she called, though she doubted she would see the loft anytime soon. As she let herself into her own cabin and hung her cloak on the wall, Elizabeth realized that she regarded Louisa as a well-intentioned and kind woman.

The rain continued throughout the next two days. Jacob stayed at the blockhouse a good share of the time. It was probably for the best, since Elizabeth's relationship with him still seemed strained, but it made her feel glum; Jacob seemed as involved as ever with his uncle. Aside from those concerns, she wondered what was going on in the cabin across the way.

When the rain stopped and the sun finally reappeared on the third morning, Elizabeth determined she would visit her aunt whether Sallie wanted to see her or not. She piled a plate full of jumbles she'd made with hickory nuts the day before, placed a napkin over the top, and started across the settlement to Louisa's old cabin. She stood before the door a moment, took a deep breath, and rapped several times. Soon, the door opened an inch and Sallie peered out at her.

Elizabeth forced a smile onto her lips. "Good morning, Aunt Sallie, I've brought you some cookies. May I come in?"

"I'd rather you didn't, Elizabeth," she replied, and started to close the door.

Elizabeth wedged her toe in between the door and

the jamb. "Don't shut me out, Aunt Sallie. Please, I'd like to talk with you. Can't you see me for a few minutes?"

"We've nothing to say to each other, Elizabeth." Sallie opened the door a few inches. "Seems our husbands have done all the talking that's necessary, and that took place down in Detroit."

"You're not in Detroit anymore, Aunt Sallie, and you're going to need help in order to survive up here. Let's talk about it, all right?"

Sallie hesitated. Her eyes moved from Elizabeth's earnest expression to the plate she held in her hands. The scowl on her face softened as she relented and opened the door wide enough for Elizabeth to step inside.

"All right. Come in, but I can only let you stay for a few minutes. I've got to get back to work with Isaac soon, or he'll wonder where I am."

Elizabeth set the cookies in the center of the table, pulled out a chair, and seated herself. Sallie called Amy and Sarah over, offered each of them a cookie, and sent them off to play, then sat across the table from Elizabeth.

She stared at the remaining cookies for a moment before dropping the napkin over them once more and shoving them toward her niece. "They look wonderful, Elizabeth, but you'd better take what's left back home for Jacob."

Elizabeth shook her head. "I brought them for your family, and I won't take them back."

Sallie went to the hearth and retrieved the pan in which Elizabeth had brought her the flapjacks, then sat again. "I'd like to return this to you. You'll be needing it, I'm sure. I apologize for returning it empty, I know it's not polite, but in my circumstances, I'm sure you understand."

Elizabeth nodded.

"Now," Sallie continued, "what is it you've come here to say? You'd best be out with it."

Elizabeth was hurt by her aunt's abrupt nature, and spoke quickly. "Aunt Sallie, don't shut me out of your life. Please let's get to know each other again."

Sallie's mouth set in a hard line. "I'm afraid I know all I want to about you and your husband, Elizabeth."

"But you're letting such bitterness rule your life."

"Wouldn't you be bitter if every penny you'd saved for the past eight years was spent for a piece of land you hated? Wouldn't you be bitter if, in order to save that money, you'd had to hide it between the floorboards, behind cupboards, in ceiling cracks in order to keep your husband from wasting it?" Sallie buried her face in her hands.

Elizabeth touched her aunt's wrist, but Sallie shook her hand away before she continued.

"There's more. Isaac is a good man. A hardworking man. He's provided for me, his boys, our girls. We haven't ever had much, but we've always had enough. Then, when I'd put enough by, I talked him into moving West. He didn't want to move, but I told him how much better our life would be. He's not the most educated man in the world, but he's got his pride. At least, he *had* some pride, until he got taken by Will Morgan." Sallie dropped her eyes.

Elizabeth remained silent while her aunt collected herself.

With a sigh and a shrug, Sallie looked up. "There. Now I've said more than I wanted to, and I don't care much what you think, because there's nothing you can do to change things. Now you'd best be on your way." She rose from her chair.

Elizabeth got up. "Not just yet. I haven't finished what I came here to say. Now that you're in Riverton, you could make it a lot easier on yourself if you'd let the rest of the community get a little closer to you, rather than trying to keep everyone at such a distance. As for Isaac's pride, you'd better tell him there's not a one of us in Riverton that didn't fall prey to some flowery description of Will Morgan's about his land. Even Jacob.''

Sallie's face registered shock. "I don't believe it. Surely Jacob knew what he was getting into before he brought you here.''

Elizabeth shook her head. "Nothing could be further from the truth.''

"Then why did you stay?''

Elizabeth shrugged, as a surprising realization formed into words. "I guess we've come to believe in this town. It's going to be something some day, but only if we stay when the times get rough.'' She spoke as if in a dream. Could her feelings truly have changed that much? Perhaps there *was* hope her aunt could learn to adjust, too.

Sallie's head moved slowly from side to side. "If we had the money, we'd have been gone the day after we arrived. As it is, we're stuck until we can find someone who wants to buy this land. That opportunity's not likely to come until spring, at the earliest, which means an entire wretched winter living in a forest too thick to let the sunshine through.''

"That being the case,'' Elizabeth concluded, "you'd better make the most of what you've got for the time being, including helpful neighbors. Don't turn anybody's help away—especially not Will Morgan's. Besides, any improvements will make your land more valuable when you sell.''

Sallie nodded slowly.

Elizabeth stepped to the door and opened it. "I won't keep you any longer.'' She squeezed her aunt's hand and added, "Remember, I still love you as much as I did when I was a child and you were taking care of me. You were practically my mother for seven years, and I'll never forget that.'' She blinked back a tear.

"Good day, Elizabeth,'' Sallie managed as her voice cracked with emotion.

Later that afternoon, Elizabeth went with Mrs. Clarke to the Pierce's Mercantile in Upper Saginaw. Mrs. Clarke helped Elizabeth order material for curtains for her new home, and other miscellaneous articles she would need for her fireplace and kitchen.

Jacob had made an extra effort to be considerate of Elizabeth since their return from Detroit, and at times it seemed that everything was normal between them. Then, she would recall her bitter disappointment over what had happened in Detroit, and would pull back from him again. Most of the time, she managed to hide her unhappiness over the fact that Jacob was still deeply involved in business with his uncle. She worked hard at doing just that when Jacob came home a few days later for supper with some news.

"Uncle Will wants to organize a cabin raising for the Knights, but Isaac told him to go jump in the river! How's that for gratitude?" He took his place at the table while Elizabeth began serving dinner.

"Coming from him, it doesn't surprise me," Elizabeth said. "I can't blame Isaac if he's still bitter about the land deal, but he's foolish not to take anyone's help. I got the impression Aunt Sallie only moved into the cabin because of her daughters. Of course, after Will practically had to tie Isaac down just to keep from getting shot, I should think things might have gotten worse between them."

"Surprisingly, Isaac's softened by a degree or two since that day," Jacob said. "Now, he just tells Will to stay away without bothering to pick up his gun. Of course, once Will says what he's come to say, Isaac tells him not to interfere. At least that's what he said about the cabin raising."

"How did Will respond?"

"He told Isaac he was a fool, that he should be grateful and go along with it, even if he *was* opposed to letting anyone set foot on his land." Jacob chewed on a piece of venison steak, then reached across the

135

table for Elizabeth's hand. "Elizabeth, would you do something? Would you talk to your aunt and see if she can convince that stubborn husband of hers to let the rest of the world in?"

Elizabeth pulled her hand away to cut a piece of meat. "If 'the rest of the world' includes Will Morgan, I don't think it will do any good. I've already suggested she accept help—especially Will's—but I got the feeling it didn't change her outlook any."

"You're still blaming him, aren't you?" Jacob's tone revealed his irritation.

"Who am I supposed to blame, Jacob?"

Jacob shoved his chair back, making a loud scraping noise. "Will's trying to help them out. At least give him credit for that. Isaac Knight's making it awfully tough for anyone in Riverton to get anywhere near him. Will just thought it would bring the community together if we all pitched in and helped with their cabin."

"Will should have thought about being more honest in the first place, then none of these problems would have come up," Elizabeth retorted, setting her fork down with a clank.

"You'll never let go, will you?" Jacob asked, rising from the table. "You're going to hold that against Will for—"

"—for as long as it takes him to realize he has to start putting honesty before profit," Elizabeth finished as she stood up to face him. "I'll feel different about him when he mends his ways."

"And what about me? When will you feel different about me? There's been a distance between us since we came back from Detroit."

She spoke slowly, quietly. "In spite of my love for you, which is considerable, Jacob Morgan, I will only respect you if you uphold honesty in your business transactions."

"I've already promised you I would, but you don't seem to believe me."

"I believed you when you said you wouldn't get involved in your uncle's bank, and look what happened. Why should I believe you now?"

Without answering, Jacob turned and walked out of the cabin.

As much as he hated to admit it, Elizabeth was right, Jacob thought to himself as he strolled in the darkness along the bank of the Saginaw River near his new home. Somehow, he hadn't realized how his sense of values had slipped; how strictly she believed in honesty and forthrightness. He didn't want a marriage devoid of respect. How empty her love for him would seem if she couldn't respect him as well.

Jacob sat on the bank and looked across the moonlit river. Perhaps he had been wrong in thinking the Lord wanted him involved in that venture. *No*, he admitted, *that was my own selfish desire, not the Lord's leading.* He would have to do the right thing. He would have to find an investor to buy him out; and that might prove impossible.

Jacob went on walking, and thinking, mulling over the situation. "At least I can be honest in my attempts to sell land," he mumbled to himself.

Feeling the need for guidance from a power greater than himself, Jacob dropped to his knees on the grassy riverbank.

"Father in heaven, thank you for all the blessings you've given me. Lord, I want to do what's right, but sometimes I go wrong. I thought you wanted me to invest in Uncle Will's bank, but I see now I've been confusing my own desires with what you truly want for me. And Lord, I need to ask your forgiveness. I've sinned, but of course, you already know that. I should have spoken up when Will sold the land to Isaac Knight. I should have told him the truth, but I kept quiet, and that was wrong. Please forgive me, and guide me, Father in heaven, so I can please you, and serve you, in Jesus' name, Amen."

Jacob stood up, and resumed his walk by the river. He had gone quite a way when he started thinking about a man he had recently met in Upper Saginaw, a fellow named Zachary Fenmore, who was visiting his wife's relatives, the Pierces. He wondered why he should be thinking about Fenmore.

Suddenly, he knew why. "Thank you, Lord," Jacob whispered, and smiled at the way God had answered his prayer.

Back when Will had first solicited partners to fund the banking ventures, the others couldn't even afford to go ahead with it unless Jacob invested, too. This rich Fenmore fellow appeared on the scene from the East coast, and wanted to put his money into a small town banking venture, but Will had preferred to keep the investors local. Jacob was sure Zachary Fenmore would jump at the chance to buy his shares in the Riverton Bank.

Jacob thought about the price of land, and knew he would like to invest in more. Of course, once he sold his shares in the bank, he would have to use his recovered investment to pay off his bank mortgage, because the bank wouldn't carry a mortgage for a nonshareholder. But, if Zachary Fenmore would agree to hold his mortgage, he could use the capital to buy farmland he was certain he could resell next spring at a decent profit. Elizabeth had opposed the mortgage, but Jacob could meet the payments until summer was over, when he would have plenty of extra money from land sales to pay it off.

As for his land deals, Jacob realized that honesty would be the easy part, but the selling could get mighty tough. He would have considered offering some of his Riverton parcels to the Fenmore fellow, but Uncle Will did not want any of those lots going to people who would not settle down here, and Jacob was bound by the terms of his purchase from his uncle to abide by that wish. Fenmore had already made it clear he would never move to Michigan, and Will wanted buyers who were coming to stay, not opportunists coming to make the price of land so high settlers could not afford it.

Jacob decided not to worry about selling any land right now. The Lord would guide him in it. Besides, the best time would be next spring, when a new onslaught of immigrants would be making their way into Detroit. With so many fresh off the steamers and ready to buy a piece of property, he shouldn't have any trouble selling the Riverton lots he had bought from Uncle Will, and the farmland he would buy with his recovered bank investment as well. Maybe it could work out. Maybe he could use his business sense the way the Lord intended—not just to line his own pockets.

The following morning dawned bright and sunny, but Elizabeth arose with a sense of despair. Jacob had been gone until late the previous evening, returning sometime after she had already gone to bed. Now he barely said two words at breakfast. He seemed preoccupied, too deep in thought over something to be questioned about what was on his mind.

Aside from the troubling discussion last night and Jacob's quietness this morning, Elizabeth had determined she must once again face her aunt and try to persuade her to become more open to assistance from others in the community. Elizabeth thought her effort might be a futile one, as she had told Jacob when he had asked her to talk with her aunt, but she must make the effort, nonetheless. Sallie and Isaac were only hurting themselves and their children by carrying on with their resentments.

Elizabeth wrapped a shawl around her shoulders and headed for Louisa's cabin. When she arrived, no one was there. She dreaded talking to both Sallie and Isaac, though she knew that was what must be done.

She headed for their cabin site, trying to form in her mind the most logical arguments she could think of. When she stepped to the edge of their lot, she was disheartened at how much more work would be needed before they would finish their cabin. A few more logs had been prepared and stacked, but it would take weeks for Sallie and Isaac to finish.

Isaac shouted to Elizabeth the moment he saw her. "Leave us be. Can't you see we got work to do?" He swung his ax.

Sallie paused as she hauled branches, and Elizabeth sensed her aunt would have spoken to her if it hadn't been for Isaac's interference.

Elizabeth started toward them, calling out, "I want to talk with both of you. It's very important, and it won't take long."

Isaac yelled, "I told you, get away. We don't wanna hear anything you got to tell us." He set his ax aside to twist a branch off the felled tree trunk. "Besides, we got no time for talk if we're gonna get our cabin up."

Elizabeth stood a few feet away. "That's what I came to see you about. You'll freeze to death before you get that cabin finished unless you accept some help."

Isaac spoke in angry tones. "Will Morgan sent you here, didn't he? Well, you can just tell that cuss to mind his own business. We'll do fine by ourselves. We don't want no part of this community. We're movin' come spring. Now go on home." When he turned to pick up his ax again, Elizabeth quickly moved between him and the log.

Isaac looked up, stunned, and red-faced with anger.

Elizabeth confronted him. "You've already become a part of this community by staying in Louisa's cabin—"

Isaac cut her off. "You're wrong. Me an' my boys haven't stepped foot there, rain or shine. Sallie used it 'cause of the girls an' that's all."

"Then all the more reason to get your cabin up. Don't you want you family all under one roof?"

Isaac sputtered to himself.

Elizabeth went on. "If you care in the least about your wife and children, you'll accept the help of your neighbors in raising your cabin. The ground will be hard and white before you and Sallie can finish."

"You don't scare me none," Isaac ground out through clenched teeth.

Sallie spoke up. "Elizabeth's right, Isaac. We need help, for the sake of the children."

"No. I made a mistake buyin' this land, but I'll make it right. You'll see," he insisted.

Elizabeth continued. "Why make your wife and children suffer while you purge yourself? Why not watch the sweat roll off Will Morgan's brow while he works on your cabin? You're the one who will benefit, when you go to sell next spring. Don't you want to profit off of his hard work?"

Isaac started to speak, then seemed to catch a glimpse of what Elizabeth had proposed.

Sallie spoke up, "That's true, Isaac. Let's put him to work. And once we've got the cabin up, we can go on with other chores."

Isaac glanced at the pile of logs he had stripped for his cabin, then back to Elizabeth. "All right. You tell Will Morgan I'll let him and the others in here to build the cabin, but it's only 'cause of the children, you understand."

"I understand," Elizabeth answered.

CHAPTER 11

ELIZABETH WENT TO THE NEW HOUSE to look for Jacob. She thought it best if he tell Uncle Will that the Knights had agreed to a cabin-raising. When she arrived at the site, she couldn't find Jacob anywhere, so headed toward the blockhouse, assuming he was working with his uncle. The blockhouse door was partially opened when she arrived, so she stepped inside. Except for the glow of a lantern off in a back corner, the blockhouse was dark.

"Jacob?" she called, heading toward the light.

She heard scuffling and stepped toward the sound. "Jacob, are you in here?" The scuffling noise grew louder. She strained her eyes to see in the wan light, and could barely make out Will draping a large piece of canvas over something bulky.

He finally answered. "Elizabeth, stay right there. I'll be with you in a minute." He finished his shuffling and came toward her. "Elizabeth, is something wrong?" he asked, guiding her back through the door and outside again, as if trying to keep her away from the object he had just covered.

His suspicious actions made her want to ask him about it, but she was still too disgruntled with him and decided to keep the exchange as brief as possible. "Isn't Jacob here?"

"I haven't seen him today. If I do, I'll tell him you're looking for him."

Elizabeth thought for a moment. "No need. I just came to tell you the Knights have agreed to accept help on their cabin."

Will's bushy brows raised as his eyes gleamed with delight. "Good work, Elizabeth. I knew if anyone could talk sense into that bunch, you could." He gave her a warm smile of approval. "I'd better start organizing the menfolk. We'll give them the best cabin-raising Riverton's ever seen."

Elizabeth did not return his smile. "I have to get back to my work," she responded curtly, and strode away.

Later that morning, Elizabeth worked over the hearth fire, hoping earnestly her gingerbread would rise as it should. She was pleased when she thought of her small success with Isaac and Sallie, and hoped relationships would soon improve between them and the rest of the Riverton residents.

At a little past noon, the cabin door opened. She glanced up to be certain it was Jacob, then began serving dinner on the plates she had already set out. She wondered if he would still be as sullen and quiet as he had been at breakfast.

She returned to the fireplace, swung out the crane, and replaced her pot on the hook. As she did, she felt Jacob's arms wrap around her. She held still, relishing the secure feeling of his embrace.

He whispered in her ear, "Thank you. I love you, Elizabeth."

She turned to face him. "Will must have told you about Isaac," she conjectured.

He laid a hand alongside her cheek. "I appreciate

143

what you did today. I know it couldn't have been easy confronting Isaac the way you did."

"After he agreed to the cabin-raising, I came to tell you, but you weren't at the new house, so I went to the blockhouse looking for you. That's when I told Will."

"The way you feel about Uncle Will, I know that wasn't easy, either, but I'm glad you talked to him. He's already out rounding up volunteers." Jacob rested his forehead against hers for a moment, then glanced at the dinner table. "Let's sit down and eat while your dinner is hot. We should talk." He pulled out a chair for her, then sat and gave thanks.

"Jacob, where were you this morning?" Elizabeth wondered. "Will said he hadn't seen you."

Jacob swallowed a bite of hash and smiled. "I'm glad you asked, because I have some very good news."

"Oh?"

"You were perfectly right to make the point you did last night about honesty in my business dealings. I've thought about it, and prayed about it ever since we left Detroit, and came to some decisions last night I think will please you."

Elizabeth reached for his hand. "I hope your decisions are not simply a gesture to make me happy."

"You needn't worry. They are my own, with the Lord's guidance. First of all, I sold my shares in Uncle Will's bank this morning to an investor in Upper Saginaw."

She took in a sharp breath. "Oh, Jacob, I'm glad," she uttered.

"Also, I'm going to be upright and honest when I go to Detroit next spring to sell my land. I'll get some maps printed up . . ."

At her questioning look he continued quickly. "Not the kind of maps you're thinking of, Elizabeth.

144

Accurate maps that show what's really in Riverton. No Paper Towns for me."

She clasped her hands together, pressed her eyes closed, and silently thanked her Lord, then looked up at her husband. "Jacob, I'm so happy."

He placed his hands around hers. "Elizabeth, there's one more thing." His tone became serious. "Have you really forgiven me for my part in Uncle Will's land deal with Isaac Knight? You can't know how much I regret the hurt I caused you and them. I need to know whether you really have forgiven me."

Tears formed in Elizabeth's eyes as she tried to find her voice to speak. "Oh, yes, Jacob," she managed in a half-whisper, "I really have forgiven you."

As the afternoon passed, Elizabeth felt more in love with Jacob than she ever had before, and she was certain that soon, her faintest doubts would vanish.

Word quickly passed around the settlement that the men would soon raise a cabin for the Knights. Clara Langton organized the feminine efforts, checking with all the ladies to see that a variety and abundance of homecooked dishes would be prepared, with plenty of extra helpings for the hard-working men. Two weeks later, the Knights' cabin-raising began.

Though there was some awkward tension at first, Elizabeth noticed that Isaac and his sons soon blended into the background while letting Will organize the work.

Aunt Sallie remained on the periphery with her two daughters while the ladies organized their outdoor kitchen. Elizabeth knew most of the women, but a few had come from Upper Saginaw whom she hadn't seen before.

Children of all ages romped around. Several boys played with a ball one of them had brought, while the girls mothered their rag and cornhusk dolls.

Elizabeth tended to her chowder, then approached

the three reluctant participants, who lingered near their hut.

"Aunt Sallie, Amy, Sarah, wouldn't you like me to introduce you to some of the ladies, and their children?"

The blond girls looked down, and Sallie stroked their hair while coaxing them. "Girls, I think it's time we make some new friends, don't you?"

Amy shook her head. "I don't want new friends. I've got Sarah to play with."

Sallie tipped her daughter's chin up. "Amy, we're going to be living here for several months. You could get lonely without any friends."

"I don't care. I hate it here," she cried, and ran off to the corner of the hut.

Sarah looked at her mother. "I hate it here, too!" she echoed, then ran to join her sister.

Sallie watched her go, then turned to Elizabeth. "I guess they're not ready for new friends yet, but I'd like to meet the ladies, if you don't mind."

Elizabeth smiled, and breathed a small sigh of relief as she led her aunt to the gathering of ladies.

Most of the women had set their hot dishes by a pit fire to keep warm, and now tended to some sewing, chatting as they worked. Elizabeth introduced her aunt to Mae Clarke, Clara Langton, Mary Stone, and Emma Farrell. A very young woman from Upper Saginaw, who was a stranger to Elizabeth, introduced herself as Dolly Claxton, and Louisa Morgan needed no introduction.

Clara Langton introduced a well-dressed woman sitting beside her, a late arrival whom Elizabeth had never met. "Elizabeth, Sallie, this is Mrs. Zachary Fenmore, a cousin to the Gordon Pierce's of Upper Saginaw," she said with an air of importance. "Mr. Fenmore is looking into investments while his wife visits her relatives. They've come all the way from Portsmouth, New Hampshire. Mr. Pierce insisted she come to the cabin raising with him while her husband tends to business, since she hasn't been to one before."

Elizabeth smiled at the woman. "Pleased to meet you," she said, thinking Mrs. Fenmore's silk finery seemed out of place among the array of calico and gingham that surrounded her.

Sallie simply nodded, then followed Elizabeth to an empty space on a plank bench where they could easily participate in the women's conversation. For a while, they listened to Mrs. Fenmore tell about life in Portsmouth, New Hampshire. Eventually, conversation turned to concerns much closer to Riverton. Though Sallie said little at first, she gradually warmed to the fellowship of those who surrounded her, and explained how she and Elizabeth had become close during Elizabeth's childhood.

After a while, the women swung into action, serving a dinner from all the dishes they had brought to the clearing. There were many dishes of baked beans, ham, corn, homemade bread, hickory nut cakes, apple pies, and several jugs of fresh cider. Afterward, the men mingled in groups, talking about business, or how the weather had affected the crops of those who had been living in the area long enough to have harvested their planting. When Elizabeth had finished cleaning up, she looked for Jacob. She soon saw that he was involved in a discussion with several other men, so she strolled off by herself, content to be away from the women's talk for a few minutes. As she neared a group of men from Upper Saginaw, she overheard fragments of conversation.

A tall, lean man spoke. "Word is out that the Riverton Bank issued over $5,000 in notes, but they've only got $2,500 in gold and silver to back it up. I heard they really overstated the value of that land. The bank directors pledged to capitalize it, too."

His stout companion commented, "I tell you, I

wouldn't touch one of them bank notes. It's all gonna come crashin' down on 'em some day.''

A fellow in patched overalls interjected, "Yup, I reckon yur right 'bout that. Why, jest last week Harvey Northrup told me that new bank over there in Genesee County was lookin' mighty shaky, 'bout to fold up, he claims.''

The tall gentleman spoke again. "It only takes a few to start a run on a bank. Once that happens, a bank is finished.''

His friend in overalls started on a different tack, and Elizabeth moved away, thinking about what she'd heard, wondering if it was true that the bank had issued twice as many notes as it had deposits on hand. "Sounds just like Will Morgan," she mumbled to herself. How thankful she was that Jacob had decided to sell his share.

She heard footsteps behind her. "Pardon? You talking to yourself, my dear wife?" Jacob teased.

"Oh, Jacob, it's you.''

He slipped his arm about her waist. "Working on this cabin makes me realize how thankful I am that the carpenters have nearly finished with the downstairs of our home. A week from now, we can move in. We'll be a little short on furniture for a while. Can you make do?''

Elizabeth nodded. "I don't have the yard goods for our curtains yet," she mentioned. "When I get them, it will take me some time to do the hemming.''

"Mrs. Pierce sent word with Mr. Pierce that everything you ordered a while back came in yesterday. I'll finish paying him for it before he goes home tonight, then he'll bring it along when he comes tomorrow morning." Jacob turned to glance at the walls that the men had started putting up in the Knights' clearing. "One more day of work on this cabin, and we'll be done raising it," he commented. "You can start on your curtain sewing tomorrow right

148

here. I'll bet some of the other ladies would be glad to help you when you're not tending to meals."

Elizabeth's attitude brightened. She knew, with her limited sewing experience, she could use many helping hands if she was to have her curtains ready in a week's time. Later, she asked some of the women if they would be interested in helping her with them the next day, and many were glad to offer assistance. When some of them expressed interest in seeing her home, she led them down the trail, and showed them through the first floor rooms.

Dolly Claxton commented enthusiastically when she saw it. "Well, I never would've guessed a young couple could have afforded such a place right off."

Mrs. Fenmore spoke out. "Oh, don't get the wrong impression, Dolly, this house isn't paid for. My husband agreed to personally hold a sizable mortgage on it when he bought Jacob Morgan's bank stock." She stepped past Elizabeth with her nose in the air.

Throughout the remainder of the afternoon, Elizabeth felt that old queasiness coming back, the nervous realization that her happiness lay not so much in the knowledge that she would soon occupy the new home Jacob was building for her, but in believing he had paid for it. To learn that Mr. Fenmore held a large mortgage on the new house, to discover that Jacob had not told her, but that people who had been strangers to her until that day talked about it freely in front of others, hurt her deeply.

She planned to ask Jacob about it that night, but by the time they came home from the cabin-raising, it was too late, and he was too tired from a day of hard work to do anything but drop into bed.

The following day, the ladies helped hem Elizabeth's curtains. Mrs. Fenmore, though she had wanted to see the house in which the curtains would hang, did not offer to do any sewing, and Elizabeth assumed she had always lived in circumstances where a seamstress or hired woman had done all the sewing. Elizabeth found it difficult to keep from showing her worry as she placed stitch after stitch into her hems. From time to time, she watched the men raise the logs into place, observed the expert notching Will performed where the corners met, and prayed for the cabin-raising to soon be over. By day's end, the cabin was up, her curtains were hemmed, and she was glad to return home.

But again, Jacob dropped into bed too exhausted to talk, and Elizabeth realized any discussions would have to wait one more day.

The next morning, a Sunday bright with rare October sunshine, brought Elizabeth the perfect chance to ask him about the mortgage. She prepared a fine breakfast of browned sausage, stack cakes, and eggs, and waited until Jacob had set his fork down before easing into the topic.

"I met a Mrs. Fenmore at the house-raising," Elizabeth began, "and she shared a most interesting bit of information with several of the ladies who were there."

Jacob laid his napkin alongside his plate and moved his chair back before responding. "I imagine she was full of talk about the East. I'd met her husband a while back, and learned they were visiting from New Hampshire," he explained.

"She did speak of life in Portsmouth, but what I'm referring to relates closer to home." She paused.

"Well, Elizabeth, go ahead. Tell me what she said that was so interesting," he urged. "Reverend Clarke will be starting the worship service soon, and I should help the others set out the benches."

Elizabeth went on. "Mrs. Fenmore informed several of the ladies, including myself, that her husband holds a sizable mortgage on our new house."

Jacob's face reddened. "She had no right to say that. That mortgage is a private matter between me and her husband."

"Why, Jacob? Why did you mortgage the house? I know you could have paid for it with the endowment your father gave you."

Jacob let out a sigh of anger and frustration. "Elizabeth," he began, leaning across the table, "sometimes I wish you were more like other women, and neither knew nor cared about your husband's business affairs."

"But I'm not. Jacob, why owe money to someone when you don't have to? Wouldn't you feel better, knowing you owned our home, that nothing could happen to take it away from us?"

He stood and paced across the cabin floor. "Elizabeth, stop worrying. Nothing will happen," he placated.

"How can you be so sure?" she challenged.

He sat down again. "I'll explain it to you. First of all, I have enough hard cash money left from the endowment to make the payments until the end of next summer. Second of all, in the spring, I'm going to sell my Riverton lots, and some farmland I bought as an investment. I'll go to Detroit when the immigrants start coming in, close some deals, recover my investment and make an honest profit, and that will be the end of it. We'll be much better off doing it my way, I guarantee."

She stood up abruptly. "You'd better go see if the others need your help getting ready for the church service. I'll be along shortly."

When Jacob had gone, Elizabeth thought about what he had said. He seemed so confident that things would work out. If only she could be so sure. She sent up a little prayer. "Lord Jesus, please guide Jacob in everything he does, and give me enough love and understanding to accept whatever the future holds for us. Amen."

Over the next few days, Elizabeth tried to shove her concerns over Jacob's debt to the back of her mind. Finally, moving day arrived, and even mortgage worries could not dampen her enthusiasm for living in their new home. Jacob and Will carried their few belongings from the LaMore cabin: bedding, two trunks, and a few utensils for the fireplace and cooking. Then they worked together adding fixtures above the windows so she could hang her curtains.

As Will helped Jacob with the last curtain rod, she held up one of the newly hemmed curtains, imagining how it would look at the window.

Will glanced in her direction and commented. "I expect you'll have this place lookin' like home in no time."

"I expect," she answered, folding the curtain and laying it aside.

When the last rod was in place, Jacob spoke to her. "While you work on unpacking your chests and hanging curtains, Will and I are going down to the blockhouse. We'll be back a little later for something hot to drink. How about perking some of that coffee you've been saving for a special occasion, if you think you can manage it in that fancy new fireplace of yours," he teased.

"Jacob . . ." Elizabeth paused, "I don't mean this as a criticism, but until Papa ships our furniture, this house will look awfully bare. We haven't even a table to eat from."

"Don't worry, Elizabeth. Your furniture should come before winter sets in. Until then, we'll make do. We can always eat off the top of one of your trunks."

When she was alone again, Elizabeth built the first fire in her new fireplace and set her coffee perking as Jacob asked. She emptied one trunk and slid it in front of the fireplace where it could serve as a table.

Looking around, she realized that curtain hanging should be done next, to make the first floor look more like home. The upstairs was still unfinished, and remained closed off. Jacob had released the carpenters from Detroit for the winter months, saying he would hire them back come spring.

She began hanging her new curtains at the windows in front, first, and was hanging the second curtain when she spotted Jacob and Will carrying something huge and canvas-covered toward the house. She left her curtain dangling, half hung, and hurried to open the door for them.

They made their way inside and set the burden down, then Will eyed the trunk in front of the fireplace with disdain. "That has got to go," he concluded as he approached it.

Jacob joined him, nodding agreement. "Elizabeth, where do you want us to put it?"

Puzzled, and slightly annoyed, she looked from Will to Jacob. "I want you to leave it where it is so I can serve you coffee," she reasoned.

Will shook his head slowly. "That'll never do for coffee," he informed her, then looking at Jacob, added, "will it, Jacob?"

"Indeed, no," he agreed.

Elizabeth suppressed her mounting ire. "Jacob, you just told me a short while ago to use a trunk for a table."

Will lifted one end of the trunk as Jacob hefted the other end into the air. With a groan, Will asked again, "Where to, Elizabeth?"

Baffled, but unwilling to argue, she looked hurriedly for a different spot, then pointed to a corner of the parlor. As they moved the trunk to the next room, she walked over to the bulky item Jacob and Will had just carried in, wondering if Jacob had made her a piece of furniture. It would be fitting, she thought, if he had wanted to surprise her with something they needed such as a table. She would cherish anything he had crafted himself out of his love for her. Reaching for the canvas, she was about to uncover the mysterious object when Will startled her.

"Stand back, Elizabeth. You just be patient for another minute."

She stepped away, watching while they jockeyed their cargo to approximately the space the trunk had occupied.

"Now, you can take off the cover," Will told her.

She hesitated, looking at Jacob for confirmation. When he nodded encouragement, she grasped the heavy canvas and tugged until it slowly slid back, revealing one end of a polished oak table. The grain of the wood was dark and rich, with a finish that glowed softly in the daylight.

Elizabeth gasped when she saw it. "Jacob, thank you." She ran her fingertips over the grain, thinking of the hours he must have spent making this special surprise in time for their move.

"Thank Will," he corrected. "It's his handiwork."

Will spoke up, "I was working on this the other day when you came looking for Jacob at the blockhouse. I'm hopin' you'll put aside your hard feelings toward me, Elizabeth."

She jerked her head up. "You're giving me this table as some sort of peace offering?" she asked, her volume increasing with her anger. "Well, you can just take this table right out of here, Will Morgan, because as long as you're dishonest in your business deals, I'll have nothing to do with it." She redraped the canvas over the exposed end with a yank. "I hope some day, you'll realize that your paper town and your paper banknotes are but paper promises of what Riverton could be if you were honest!"

CHAPTER 12

NEARLY APRIL. Elizabeth thought, as she watched drops of melting snow fall from the roof past the front window. The warmer temperature chased away memories of the snowstorms that had brought the Knights and Morgans together in front of Jacob's blazing fires. He had become an expert at keeping the first floor cozy, and at disarming the Knights' objections to staying over when their cabin would have been too cold for sleeping comfortably. The tension between the families had eased considerably.

Elizabeth glanced about the still bare rooms of her new home. Her father's shipment of furniture had not arrived before the shipping lanes closed for the winter, and she was tired of the few pieces of crude cabin furniture she and Jacob had been using for the last six months. At least she had a small, rough table in front of the fireplace, instead of a trunk. She was thankful for that.

The oak dining table Uncle Will had given her the first day they had moved into the house went back out the door following her outburst, and she had not seen

Will since. It was just as well their paths had not crossed. She still resented him for duping her relatives. The few times she had seen Louisa, awkward moments had resulted for both. Louisa seemed never to have seen anything wrong with the way her husband did business, and seemed to blame Elizabeth for not getting along with Will.

Throughout the winter, church services had been held in Elizabeth and Jacob's home. By arranging the portable benches, which had previously been used outdoors, Elizabeth and Jacob accommodated those in the community who wished to attend Sunday services in their parlor and common rooms.

Elizabeth rested her hand on her swollen abdomen as her baby stirred. Never had she felt so clumsy and awkward as she did now, and she was anxious for the day when she could carry her infant in her arms. Aunt Sallie had predicted that by the first of April her baby would be born. *It couldn't come soon enough to suit me,* Elizabeth thought.

Elizabeth yearned for the day the ice would be melted in Lake Erie to allow the season's shipping to begin. The river had already thawed, and Jacob had been gone all morning with Will in a canoe to check his traps. Elizabeth looked forward to his return. In a few weeks, he would leave for Detroit to sell his land, and she would miss the hours they shared together. She prayed time and again that he would sell his land quickly and pay off the mortgage. Hard as she tried not to worry about Jacob's debt, it still weighed on her mind. If land sales were good enough, Jacob could not only clear the debt, but rehire the carpenter to finish the upstairs. With the baby coming soon, Elizabeth would appreciate having their home finished.

The aroma from her rabbit stew had drifted pleasantly throughout the house, and she was beginning to feel hungry. As she turned toward the cabinet to get out her dishes, a mild muscle cramp made her wonder if this was the first of the pains she would endure to deliver her baby. Several minutes later, another mild pain came, and she hoped that Jacob would soon be home.

After Elizabeth had set the table, she sat by the fire to wait for her husband's return, but she soon realized that the labor pains were increasing and she would have to lie down. She waited until a pain had let up, quickly shoveled some hot coals into the fire pan, and transferred them to the bedroom fireplace where she rekindled the flame. Once the large log had caught fire, she crawled into bed and began to pray. Within moments, she heard the front door open and Jacob's voice calling her name.

On a warm and sunny day in the end of May, Elizabeth put her two-month-old son, Darius, in a fresh gown, one that had been embroidered prettily with blue and pink, and set out with Mrs. Clarke toward the Chippewa village to visit Beloved-of-the-Forest, whom she hadn't seen since the previous fall. Mrs. Clarke had been to the Indian village several times since Darius's birth, and had told Elizabeth that Beloved-of-the-Forest wished to see her and her new baby as soon as Elizabeth felt up to visiting.

The fresh, dry breeze and profusion of wildflowers blooming along the riverbank almost made up for the exceptionally wet spring that had kept Elizabeth housebound since Darius had been born. Though her arms felt a little tired from carrying her growing infant, the mile to the Indian village passed quickly, and they soon approached Beloved-of-the-Forest's lodge. When the Chippewa woman was not to be found, Mrs. Clarke inquired of her whereabouts, and some children told her she was working in her vegetable garden on the edge of the village.

As they came upon her, Beloved-of-the-Forest was

stooped over her garden row, planting seeds. When Beloved-of-the-Forest caught sight of the women, she hurried to greet them.

"It is good to see you and your little one," she spoke in English while admiring Darius. "Your son will soon grow big and strong."

"Would you like to hold him?" Elizabeth asked.

Beloved-of-the-Forest's dark eyes lit as she took Darius carefully in her arms. "He will bring you much joy, of this I am certain." She rocked the infant for a few moments, then handed him back to Elizabeth.

Following a brief conversation about the past winter, and the gentle May day, Elizabeth said, "We won't keep you from your work any longer."

Beloved-of-the-Forest asked, "You must tend your garden, too?"

Elizabeth shook her head. "I have no garden."

A look of concern filled the Chippewa woman's eyes before she responded. "You will plant garden soon as you are wise, and know the time comes when there will be no meat. Every woman here plants corn, beans, squash. I give you seeds for your garden, my friend."

Elizabeth started to protest, but kept quiet at Mrs. Clarke's nudge.

Beloved-of-the-Forest hurried to the small baskets in the garden row where she had been working, and brought seeds to Elizabeth, pouring some into each of her two apron pockets, and a third variety into Mrs. Clarke's pocket.

"When fall comes, I will show you how to save what you do not eat in summer," Beloved-of-the-Forest promised with a smile.

Elizabeth felt awkward as she responded. "Thank you. You are very kind."

Beloved-of-the-Forest raised her hand in a parting gesture, then Elizabeth followed Mrs. Clarke toward Riverton.

When they had gone a way, Elizabeth spoke. "I feel bad that Beloved-of-the-Forest gave me all these seeds. I've never had any interest in growing vegetables. Do you think someone else in the village could use them?"

"What will you tell Beloved-of-the-Forest the next time you see her and she inquires about your garden?"

"I hadn't thought about that. I was just planning on doing the same next winter as we did this past winter—buying the vegetables we wanted from the Indians' extra supplies."

They approached the village center, where Elizabeth would leave Mrs. Clarke to continue on to her home, but her friend stopped her. "Elizabeth, there won't always be extra vegetables to go around. True, the Indians did well with their hunting and trapping this year, but it isn't always so. Then they will need all the vegetables they've put by to feed their own. With more and more new settlers coming all the time, who haven't any past crop to rely on, there is an increasing reliance on what the Indians have grown, and the day will come when the Chippewas can't supply enough. I'd hate to see Darius go hungry, wouldn't you?"

A troubled expression crossed Elizabeth's features. "Maybe I should give some thought to a garden, then."

"I'll lend you my hoe and show you how to get started," Mrs. Clarke offered. "Your corn seeds are in my pocket anyway."

By the end of the afternoon, Elizabeth and Mrs. Clarke had planted and watered all of the seeds Beloved-of-the-Forest had given them, and to her surprise, Elizabeth had enjoyed the effort. She stood back, viewing her plot with contentment, and looking forward to tending her garden throughout the spring and summer months.

The rocker creaked in a comforting rhythm as Elizabeth nursed Darius, who had just turned three months old. She relished this time of closeness with him, but dreaded the weeks ahead when Jacob would leave her and Darius to go to Detroit on business.

At least this June weather has been bright and cheerful, she told herself as she laid Darius in his cradle and began to prepare supper. The infant slept as Jacob shared his plans for Detroit with Elizabeth over their evening meal.

"Next week, Isaac and I are taking the steamer down to see if we can sell some land. Will's going, too. Says he needs more machinery before he can finish the mill he started building this spring."

"How long will you be gone?" Elizabeth wondered.

"That depends. If I find buyers right away, I could be home in a week's time. Otherwise, it might take a month or more."

"The furniture could arrive before you come back," Elizabeth said. "I suppose I'll be able to find some strong men to help cart it up from the dock, if you're away when it comes."

Jacob's eyebrows shot up. "I almost forgot, I have a surprise for you." He reached into his vest pocket and withdrew a letter. "This came in at the Pierce's from your father."

"I haven't heard from him since I wrote to tell him Darius had been born." Elizabeth eagerly grabbed the letter and broke the seal, then read it out loud.

Dearest Elizabeth and Jacob,

I am so proud to learn that I have a grandson, and pleased to know that you have chosen to name him after me. I hope little Darius is in good health, and wish the same for both of you.

My daughter, you are probably wondering why your furniture has not arrived. Mail delivery from Michigan is very slow. By the time I received your letter asking me to send the furniture, the shipping lanes were closed. I am truly sorry for the delay.

160

I gave my deepest consideration to circumstances as you described them in your letter of last October. While I do have my thriving medical practice here in Stockport and several real estate investments close by that require supervision, I have felt a great void in my life since your move to Michigan, and a yearning to know my only grandchild.

Your mention that there are no doctors practicing in the Riverton vicinity set me to thinking that your town has greater need of an experienced physician than does Stockport, where three of us serve the health needs of the community. After much meditation and planning, I have therefore decided to move to your town, leaving here the end of July so I will arrive in Riverton by the end of August.

With me, I shall bring all the household goods which might be of value to you in Riverton. This way, I can personally oversee their safe arrival.

When I arrive, I ask your indulgence to put me up until I can establish a residence of my own. Your description of the home you recently built led me to believe it was spacious enough to accommodate me on a temporary basis. I shall try hard not to impose.

Hattie has agreed to help me with the packing, and since she is getting on in years and has no desire to be employed by any other household, I will send her to her sister's in Syracuse with a generous pension.

Jacob's father, astute in business as he is, has agreed to oversee the sale of my properties here in New York for a fair commission, and to forward the proceeds to me in Michigan. He asked that I remember him and his household to you at this writing, and to mention that, though he is curious to know how Jacob is getting on, he has no expectation of frequent letters, since a Morgan family trait is one of avoiding correspondence.

I shall close now, with fond thoughts of our reunion to come. My love to the three of you, Papa.''

Elizabeth folded the letter carefully. Tears dampened her eyes as she looked at Jacob. "He's leaving Stockport at the end of July, Jacob, and he'll be here by the end of August. I can't believe it!"

Jacob squeezed her hand. "I'm happy for you, Elizabeth. I know how much it means to you to see him again."

"Do you mind if he stays with us, Jacob?"

"Of course not. I hope I can sell the land right away, so I can afford a carpenter to finish off the upstairs. It would be a shame to crowd your father into the downstairs with the rest of us." A frown creased his brow.

"Don't worry, Jacob, we'll make do."

Elizabeth bit the inside of her lip, and looked at Darius. He was sound asleep in his cradle. She rose from the table and stepped out the front door. Her hands were shaking as she slipped her father's precious letter into her apron pocket. She walked a few feet down the gently sloping riverbank, then sat in the grass to watch the water, knowing that with the front windows open, she could easily hear Darius if he cried.

Resting her chin in her hands, Elizabeth tried to sort out her jumbled emotions. She disliked Jacob's going away without knowing when he might return, and the news of her father's move had taken her by surprise. These circumstances must have set her on edge, she concluded.

Perhaps she wanted too much for things to be perfect when he came. She wanted him to see that Jacob was a good provider, that they lacked nothing aside from the household goods he had promised to bring. To put him up in a busy room on the first floor of the house seemed absurd.

I wish Jacob had never bought that land, she thought, *we could have finished the house with that money.*

She heard footsteps in the grass behind her and knew they were Jacob's. He sat down beside her and reached for her, taking her hand between his large, strong ones. "You know I love you, Elizabeth," he began, searching her wide brown eyes with his soft, blue ones, "and I want the very best for the three of us. I'm sorry the house isn't finished. I know that's what's bothering you, now that we've learned your father is coming to live with us."

Elizabeth rested her head on Jacob's shoulder. "You know me too well. I try not to show my feelings, but they're probably written all over my face."

Jacob nodded and grinned. "I love you just the way you are."

A lump formed in Elizabeth's throat as new tears collected in her eyes. "Oh, Jacob, I wish you didn't have to go to Detroit. I'm going to miss you more than you know."

He kissed her hair and whispered, "And I, you."

Elizabeth's garden had made a respectable start by the time Jacob left for Detroit, and she was glad to have the work of weeding it, and keeping the pests away, to take her mind off his being gone. She was outdoors watering her pumpkin patch the day after Jacob had left, when Aunt Sallie came by.

"Looks good, Elizabeth. Your seedlings are strong and healthy. I planted a garden myself, even though we might not be in Riverton long enough to reap the harvest. I figure the next people in our cabin will appreciate it."

Elizabeth set down her bucket. "Would you like to come in for some tea? I was about to take a rest and have some myself."

"Not today, thank you. I'm planning to go to Pierce's store later, and wondered if you wanted me to post any letters, or pick up any dry goods for you. I knew it wouldn't be easy for you to get there, with Jacob gone."

"Thank you for asking but I don't need anything. Your mention of letters reminds me. I haven't spoken with you since I heard from Papa last week."

163

Sallie's face clouded with uneasiness before she forced her mouth into a weak smile and casually asked, "What is the news from New York?"

"I have something surprising to tell you. Why not come in and share a cup of tea. It's been a while since we've talked."

"I guess I could take the time," Sallie admitted.

A few moments later, they sat at the small table near the fireplace.

Elizabeth opened the cover of her Bible where she had put her father's letter for safe-keeping, and handed it to her aunt.

"You might as well read this yourself. There's nothing in it I wouldn't tell you anyway."

Sallie carefully unfolded the letter and began reading while Elizabeth sipped her tea. She glanced from time to time at her aunt's face, waiting for her reaction to her father's news that he was coming to Riverton. When her aunt had read to that point, approximately a third of the way down the page, Elizabeth watched her face drain of color, and a drawn look set in about her mouth. She read the last portion of the letter over a second time, then smiled weakly as she handed it back to Elizabeth. "You must be very pleased to know he'll be here soon." Sallie's statement came out flat.

"I get so excited when I think about it, I can hardly contain myself. I'm so happy he'll be able to watch Darius grow, and Riverton will have his medical expertise. It's hard to believe I used to loathe it here! . . . But, Aunt Sallie," Elizabeth's face went grim, "you might not even see him. What if you have to move before he gets here?"

"Of course I'd be sorry . . . I mean it would be unfortunate if . . ." she stumbled over her words. "You'll be sure to tell him for me how much I regret not being able to see him, if that happens, won't you?" she finally managed.

"If you've moved, I'll be sure and tell him," Elizabeth promised. "But if you're still here—"

"We won't be," Sallie cut in. "We'll be gone by then, by the end of the summer. I'm sure we will. Isaac just has to sell our forty acres. He just has to."

An awkward moment of silence lapsed before Elizabeth spoke. "I'm sure it won't take long before Isaac has a buyer. I'll hate to see you go, but I wouldn't wish for you to be here any longer than is necessary, knowing how you feel."

Sallie shrugged her shoulders. "Much as I do want to leave Riverton, now that we've been here a few months, I have to admit that the people here have been wonderful neighbors since I've made the effort to get to know them."

Elizabeth nodded.

"Now," Sallie continued. "I'd best be on my way. Thank you for the tea. I'm off to Louisa's to ask if she needs anything, then I'll go to the Pierces."

Elizabeth walked outside with her aunt. "It's been some time since I've seen Louisa. How is she?"

"She was fine, last I saw her." Sallie looked into Elizabeth's eyes. "You and Louisa aren't on good terms now, are you? What a shame. The two of you were such good friends at one time."

Elizabeth's heart felt heavy. "I'm sorry things have turned out the way they have between us. She didn't take it well when I wouldn't let Will earn his way back into my good graces by giving me a dining table he'd made."

"But Elizabeth, it's like you told *me*. We're all living in the same small community. Don't you think it's time to put the past behind, and go on?"

"I'm waiting for him to turn the corner, to say he's done with being dishonest. I'm so afraid he'll do to someone else what he did to you. That's why I've stayed away from him. It hurts me too much to watch him take advantage of people."

"It's your decision, Elizabeth. I hope you don't let the bad feelings between you and Will go too far. It's already cost you Louisa's friendship, and in Riverton, a woman needs all the friends she can get." Sallie walked a few steps, then added, "By the way, Louisa says Will's planning to build her a fine house over in the village once his saw-mill is operating. I think she's quite excited about the prospect."

"She deserves better out of life than she's had since she moved to Riverton," Elizabeth observed.

Sallie adjusted her sunbonnet over her eyes and waved. "Call on me if you need anything."

"Thanks Aunt Sallie. I will."

As her aunt walked away, Elizabeth reflected on the cold winter nights they had spent chatting in front of the fireplace, and on their renewed friendship. She regretted that their closeness would soon end.

Elizabeth picked up her bucket and headed for the river.

Her aunt's reaction to her father's letter puzzled her, and she wondered what it was about her papa's coming to Riverton that had caused her aunt's strange reaction. Elizabeth thought back to the conversation they'd shared in the ladies' parlor in the Woodworth Hotel, and how her aunt had never explained what made her leave Stockport, except to admit it had something to do with her father.

She thought about the awkward situation between herself and Will, and the effect it had on her relationship with Louisa. She didn't like being reminded of that relationship. Nevertheless, Elizabeth was determined not to give in. Until Will Morgan told her himself he had been wrong, and had turned from his bad habit of not telling the truth, she would keep her distance.

CHAPTER 13

THE HOT JULY SUN beat down on Elizabeth's back as she struggled with a shoulder yoke, carrying buckets of water to pour on her garden. Her effort to prevent her vegetables from shriveling up in the dry weather was sapping her strength.

Jacob had been gone for a month, and she longed for his return. He was all she could think about as she worked, and she wondered when he would be able to come home to her and tell her he had sold enough land, made enough profit, to never again have to leave her for such a long time.

Isaac was still in Detroit, too, having found no one with the hard cash money to buy his farmland. Will had come home two weeks before with the machinery to finish setting up his mill. At that time, word was passed from Will, to Louisa, to Sallie, and then Elizabeth, that before he left Detroit, Isaac and Jacob were both fine, but had not found the business atmosphere to their liking.

One day faded into the next, until every day seemed the same, and she wondered if the drought would never end. It was a struggle to keep the parched ground wet enough to make her vegetables grow, scare the crows away from her corn, and prevent the rabbits from nibbling her plants away to nothing.

July closed, hot and dry, and just when Elizabeth thought she would lose her battle against nature, early August rains came pouring down, soaking into the dusty garden rows until they were flooded.

The rain continued for three days, and for the entire time, Elizabeth stayed inside, resting as much as she could to recover her strength. She napped when Darius napped, and sometimes wished for even more sleep. When the sky finally cleared, she had recovered enough energy to become restless. She missed Jacob terribly. Her heart ached that he had not been able to come home yet, and that he had not written to her. Suppose something had happened to him? She could be a widow and not even know it. At least Isaac, who could barely write his name, had managed to get word to Sallie last week that he was still attempting to sell his land and would be back as soon as possible.

"Lord, please bring Jacob home safely," she pleaded, then with more confidence, amended her prayer. "I know You will, Father in heaven. I trust Jacob to your care, and I know You won't let anything happen to him." Elizabeth felt her fears lift, but couldn't free herself of them totally.

Refreshed by the cooler air, and eager to be out of the house, Elizabeth settled Darius in her arms and headed toward her aunt's. When she arrived, Sallie was supervising her four children as they worked in her garden.

Sallie reached for Darius as Elizabeth approached her. "My, but he's growing so fast," she commented, bouncing Darius until he laughed. Amy and Sarah left their work in the garden and came to see the baby.

"Can we hold him, Mama, can we?" they asked, almost in unison.

"Go wash up, then maybe Elizabeth will let you take him," she advised. Looking at her niece, she asked, "What brings you my way?"

"Anxious to get outdoors after the rain, I guess. I'm getting a little tired of looking at the same four walls, and thought maybe you'd like to go to Upper Saginaw with me."

"Darius is quite an armload to carry that distance. I'm sure the children would enjoy watching him a while, if you don't mind leaving him with a fourteen-year-old in charge. Todd is quite good with babies. He learned young how to take care of little ones, when the girls were born."

Elizabeth glanced at Todd, who had grown taller and stronger in the months since he had come to Riverton. "I believe he could handle the job, if he wouldn't mind."

Sallie waved aside her concern. "Mind? He'd be glad to get out of the garden. Watching your little gem would be a vacation for him compared to the work he's been doing every day since Isaac went to Detroit."

When Elizabeth and Sallie started toward Upper Saginaw, Darius was being entertained by two little girls who adored him, while Todd and Charles supervised his care.

Elizabeth chatted as she walked along the trail. "I'll bet it's been hard on you, taking care of four children with Isaac gone so long. Do you have any idea when he might return?"

"No, none. Seems like he should have found someone by now who wants to live here. Have you heard from Jacob lately?"

"No, I haven't heard a word since Will came back and said both our husbands were well. I'm getting impatient to have him home again."

"I know what you mean," her aunt sympathized.

As they approached Pierce's Mercantile, Elizabeth

noticed several men gathered in front. When she neared the group, she realized that the same three men she had overheard talking the day of the cabin raising were again discussing business. She sent Sallie inside without her, then lingered by the window display as she strained to hear the men's words.

The tall, lean fellow was speaking. "Just got the word this morning, the Riverton Bank has folded up."

Elizabeth, eager to hear every word, stepped closer.

A stout fellow responded. "Folded? I'm not surprised. I knew from the start it couldn't last."

The third man, who wore patched overalls, wondered, "What's gonna happen to Will Morgan? Didn't he have the most to lose?"

The tall fellow nodded. Glancing at Elizabeth, he asked, "Say, ma'am, aren't the Morgans your kin? I seem to remember you from the cabin raising last fall up in Riverton."

"Yes, sir. My husband is Jacob Morgan. Will Morgan is his uncle."

The tall gentleman's brows moved together. "I understand Will Morgan is going to lose his mill to that Fenmore fellow from back East, and a good share of the land he pledged as a bank director. Is that right?"

Elizabeth stammered, "I . . . couldn't say. You seem to know more about the situation than I do. What else have you heard?"

The man continued. "Seems Fenmore was the most solvent of the bunch, and now he's taking advantage, buying up cheap what the others are forced to sell off." He shook his head. "Such a waste, after your husband's uncle went to all that trouble to get the mill operating."

His stout friend mused, "Guess he could use them banknotes for wallpaper, now that they're worthless."

The overalled companion agreed. "Him an' a bunch of others 'round Michigan who are goin' through the same thing. I bet there'll be 'nary a bank left, when hard times is over 'n done."

The tall man addressed Elizabeth again. "What about your husband? Was he invested in that bank?"

Elizabeth shook her head. "He sold out months ago."

The fellow in overalls wiped imaginary sweat from his brow. "Whew. Bet you're mighty glad of that."

Elizabeth nodded.

The men started on a different topic, and Elizabeth stepped inside the store, thinking about Will, and what he must be going through. Though she truly felt sorry for him, she hoped the misfortune would teach him a lesson in honesty. *Thank the Lord Jacob sold his bank shares when he did*, she thought, *now if he can just sell his land and pay off Fenmore*.

The following afternoon, Elizabeth was relaxing outside on the riverbank with Darius when her aunt came by. Sitting down beside her, Sallie spoke with a tired voice.

"Isaac's home. Got in late last night."

"What about Jacob? Did he say anything about Jacob?" she asked eagerly.

Sallie nodded. "Isaac says he's still trying to sell farmland. Jacob sends you his love, and says not to worry. He'll be home soon."

Elizabeth breathed a sigh of relief, then looking at her aunt, noticed the lines and dark circles under her eyes. "You look like you could use some rest. I bet you were up all night talking."

"I was up all night, but we only talked until about two o'clock this morning. The rest of the time I spent pacing the cabin floor, wondering how I'd survive another winter in Riverton. Isaac says he couldn't sell our farm. We have no choice but to stay."

Elizabeth's stomach lurched at the news. "Aunt Sallie, I'm so sorry. I know you must be disappointed beyond words."

Her aunt nodded, and Elizabeth could tell by the pain in her eyes that she was struggling to hold back tears.

"I suppose if you can't look forward to leaving Riverton, you can at least anticipate Papa's arrival with news of New York. He'll be here in two weeks."

As if stunned, Sallie covered her face with trembling hands. "No, no. A thousand times, no," she murmured, on the verge of tears.

Confused by her aunt's reaction, Elizabeth put her arm on her shoulders. "Aunt Sallie, what are you talking about?"

When Sallie removed her hands from her face, the look she gave Elizabeth was one of deep anguish. "I'd forgotten he was coming. I don't ever want to see him again! Never!"

"But why?" Elizabeth demanded. "Tell me why you don't want to see Papa! It has something to do with the reason you left us so many years ago, doesn't it?"

Sallie looked down, nodding. "Yes, yes it does. I'm too ashamed to talk about it."

"Surely you can tell me," Elizabeth coaxed. "You've got to talk about it. No matter what it was, I'll still love you just as much as I do now."

Sallie bit her lip, and looked into Elizabeth's eyes. "You're right. I do need to talk about it. But you've got to promise me that what I say, you'll never repeat to anyone."

"I promise. Now please, tell me why you left."

Sallie took a deep breath and began. "You know I always had the deepest respect for your Papa, Elizabeth. I enjoyed living there in his house, and you were an easy child to take care of. My life was pleasant, but gradually, things got all complicated. By that, I mean, the respect I had for your Papa—my brother-in-law—turned into something more. It turned into . . . love.''

While her aunt paused to swallow, Elizabeth struggled to keep from showing her surprise.

"Well, as time went by, I began to realize that I was getting older, and would have to marry soon, or be a spinster. I suspected that the love your Papa felt for your mother—my sister—was so deep, and lasting, he might never be able to put his first marriage behind him and think about going on with someone else. But just in case there was a tiny bit of hope, I asked to speak with him one day.'' Her lips trembled, and she paused to gain control of herself before she continued.

"Elizabeth it was awful. I never should have done it. We sat in his office, and I told him how I felt about him. He listened so patiently, so kindly, and I could even see the pain in his brown eyes, much the way I see it in yours right now. But when I was through telling him how much I loved him, and asking if there was any chance he'd ever feel the kind of love for me that he'd felt for my sister, I knew by the silence between us, I never should have approached him. I was so upset, I ran to my room, packed my bag, and took the first canal packet to Rochester.''

Elizabeth squeezed her aunt's hand between her own. "Aunt Sallie, you've nothing to be ashamed of. Aren't you glad that you asked Papa, that you didn't have to live with that question in your heart?''

"Oh, Elizabeth, if only it could have ended then and there, but it didn't. I married Isaac within weeks after I left Stockport. I still loved your Papa when I married him, but I needed a husband. I didn't know if I'd ever forget about your Papa. It took me a long time to get over him, Elizabeth. Can you understand now why I don't want to see him again?''

Elizabeth nodded.

Sallie let out a soft sob. "Elizabeth, I love Isaac, but he's nothing like your Papa was. With Isaac, we've struggled for everything we've got, even our love for one another. With your Papa, everything came so easily. I'm afraid seeing him again will bring back all those old feelings." Her hand trembled as she wiped a tear from her eye with her handkerchief.

Elizabeth spoke slowly. "I don't know what to say, Aunt Sallie, except that I'll be praying for you, and I'll leave it up to you when you want to face Papa again. Now that I know how you feel, I won't push you, but being neighbors, I suspect you're going to run into him soon after he arrives."

"I suspect you're right," Sallie said, rising.

Elizabeth picked up Darius, and walked a way with her aunt. "Things will work out, Aunt Sallie. You'll see."

"Maybe," her aunt allowed. "I'd best be getting home. Isaac's probably wondering why I've been gone so long. I'm so glad he's back, I can't tell you what a pleasure it is to have my man home, even if we *do* have to stay here another winter."

"Aunt Sallie," Elizabeth said, "you make too much of facing Papa again. Just listen to yourself. Can't you tell that what you've got with Isaac now, far exceeds that memory of a past love?"

Sallie tilted her head. "I think you've got something there, Elizabeth, I really do." With that, she hurried on her way toward her cabin, and Isaac.

For Elizabeth, the next two weeks were filled with anticipation: hoping, praying, expecting that each day, Jacob would return home; and trying to be patient while awaiting her father's arrival. Every morning after feeding Darius, she made certain her house was completely tidy and spotless. Later she would work in the garden, harvesting the vegetables as they became ripe. One day, Beloved-of-the-Forest showed Elizabeth how to dry corn, and she filled many afternoons that followed putting food by for the winter ahead.

As the last week of the month began, Elizabeth wondered for the hundredth time which day her father would arrive, and hoped his travels were going smoothly. Soon after, she was walking the riverbank with Darius when she heard a commotion at the blockhouse and dock. The river steamer was tying up, and she knew her papa had come.

Darius bounced in her arms as she ran toward the dock. When she finally caught sight of her beloved father, she stood still at the top of the riverbank and looked at him from a distance. Will was already helping to unload his freight from the steamer, and his back was to her. When he turned around and noticed her watching him, her breath caught in her throat. He stood as tall and distinguished as she remembered, in top hat and tailcoat. A cane in his right hand, and that ridiculously bright red cravat he had always worn tied about his neck. He waved, and they started toward one another, meeting where the bank and the dock came together.

"Papa, I've missed you so much," she said into his shoulder as he hugged her and Darius together.

"No more than I've missed you, my daughter." He kissed her cheek.

Elizabeth looked deep into his brown eyes, and noticed lines that weren't there before. Darius squirmed, and she turned her attention toward him. "Meet your grandson Darius. Darius, this is your grandpapa." She hitched him higher onto her hip. "Would you like to hold him, Papa?"

He reached for the child, but Darius turned away and started to cry.

Her father smiled in understanding. "No point upsetting him. We've got plenty of time to get to know one another."

The baby soon quieted down, laying his head on his mother's shoulder.

Darius Brownell looked past his daughter as he asked, "Where's Jacob?"

"He's in Detroit trying to sell some farmland he invested in a while back." When her father's eyes came back to hers, she watched his brows arch. "He's been there for two months, but should be home any day now. I'd thought he'd be here before you arrived."

Elizabeth's father looked curious, but made no comment as he turned toward the dock to check on the unloading of his belongings. Moments later, he told her, "I'd better see that these men understand they'll be well compensated for handling my freight with care. I'll be along soon. You might as well go home and wait. This will take a while."

Elizabeth hesitated. Darius started whimpering, as if he were hungry. She hated to leave, but knew her son would not be satisfied until she nursed him. "I'll see you a little later then, Papa."

Soon after Elizabeth arrived home, her Aunt Sallie came by, and sat with her while she nursed Darius. Elizabeth could tell from her aunt's edginess that she was nervous about facing her father.

With a weak smile, Aunt Sallie admitted, "I came to put old ghosts to rest. Figured I might as well get it over with right off, instead of suffering the agony of wondering what it would be like to face your papa again."

"He looks tired," Elizabeth commented. "Of course, since you last saw him, he looks much older, too."

"I'm not so worried about what changes have taken place on the *outside*, as I am on the *inside*," Sallie said.

Elizabeth nodded in understanding, and neither of them spoke again until they heard a cart approaching. She watched her aunt take a deep breath and move toward the open front door. Elizabeth stood beside Sallie as her father greeted her aunt.

"Well, Sallie, you're looking wonderfully well."

Darius Brownell took his sister-in-law's hands in his and kissed her cheek.

"Darius, you're looking fit, yourself, though I'd be less than honest if I didn't admit we're both looking somewhat older than when we last saw one another." She extracted her hands from her brother-in-law's and fussed with her bonnet strings. "I just dropped by to bid you welcome, now I've got to be on my way. I have a family of five at home, and that means no end to a woman's work."

As she stepped out the door past Darius Brownell, he laid his hand on her arm. "I'd like to meet your family one of these days soon, Sallie."

"In time, Darius, after you're settled. Good day." She gave a smile and a nod.

Elizabeth sensed a confidence in her aunt's deportment that assured her her prayers had been answered. Sallie Knight had apparently laid to rest past emotions concerning her father.

A few hours later, Darius Brownell's household goods had been unloaded from the steamer, carted to the house, and carried inside by Will Morgan and others. Elizabeth directed the men where to set each piece of furniture, speaking as little as possible to her husband's uncle. When they had finished, she could hardly get over the transformation that had taken place inside her home.

"Papa, it looks so 'lived-in.' I feel like I'm really here to stay, now that we have a dining suite, a parlor full of chairs and sofas, and chests of drawers in the bedroom." She paused to look at the daybed set up in one corner of the common room. "I'm sorry about your accommodations, but Jacob said he'll hire a carpenter to finish the upstairs after he sells his land." She looked down.

Papa slipped his arm around her waist. "Don't apologize, Elizabeth. Why don't I see about hiring someone to work on the upstairs. I've been talking

177

with Jacob's uncle. I'd never met Will Morgan before today, but he seems ambitious enough, and from what he's told me about his experiences here in Riverton, he's both qualified and in need of the work." He paused, then added, "I hope Jacob wasn't invested in that bank of his uncle's when it went under."

"No, he wasn't," she managed, between dreaded thoughts of having Will work in her house for days on end. "No need to decide right away about the upstairs, Papa."

Suddenly, she realized that be it Jacob, or her father, neither would hire the carpenters from Detroit knowing Will Morgan was available to do the work. She pushed those thoughts aside as she prepared supper.

After a few days, Elizabeth's and Darius's routines had adjusted to include Papa Brownell. Mornings, Dr. Brownell walked about the settlement, getting acquainted with the residents and learning his way around. On his first morning out, he contracted Will Morgan to finish the upstairs bedrooms, assuring Elizabeth it was the least he could do in return for his room and board. Afternoons, he took over the care of Darius as any doting grandpapa would, allowing Elizabeth time to work in her garden uninterrupted, or take solitary walks by the river where she could have time alone to think and pray.

As she ambled along the riverbank trail toward the settlement on the first day of September, her thoughts seemed limited in scope. They centered on either Jacob, or Will. As far as she was concerned, Will Morgan's work on the upstairs involved her only indirectly. Papa had hired him, and he supervised the job.

Much more pleasant was her anticipation of Jacob's arrival home. She envisioned him as he was the last time she had seen him, his wavy, golden hair tousled

178

by the breeze, his strong, tall form standing erect on the dock before he boarded the steamer for Detroit. She felt his arms around her, holding her against his firm, broad chest, and his lips against hers as he kissed her goodbye. How she longed to be in his arms again, and to taste his kisses.

She wondered how Jacob could stay away so long, and struggled to keep back worries about his well-being. "Please stay with him, protect him, and bring him safely home to me soon, Lord," she prayed so many times.

As she walked the trail toward home, she met her aunt.

"Elizabeth, I've wanted to talk with you, but haven't had much opportunity," Sallie called out as she approached. She smiled as she placed her hand on Elizabeth's shoulder. "I just wanted you to know I've been much happier since I faced your father, and put old feelings of the past behind me. I shouldn't have worried."

"I suspected that was the case. You look more cheerful than I've seen you in a long time."

"I am, Elizabeth, I am." She waved, and stepped off, "Must be on my way." Then she halted and turned. "You know," she said, "I never thought I'd say it, but now I'm mighty glad we came to Riverton!"

Elizabeth watched her aunt go, thanking her Lord for the happiness she had seen sparkling from her aunt's eyes.

When she arrived home, she noticed a tall, dapper man leaving her house. Her father shook his hand on the doorstep, then the stranger mounted a large bay gelding and rode toward Upper Saginaw. It was only the second time she'd seen a horse in Riverton. The first had been when Will Morgan had borrowed one from the Pierce's for his wedding, and it well could have been the same horse. She hastened her steps toward home, eager to learn who had been there.

"Papa, who came calling?" she asked as she stepped in the door.

Her father was playing with little Darius, and didn't look up as he answered. "Said his name is Fenmore. He came looking for Jacob."

"What did he want with Jacob?"

"He came on business. I told him Jacob was in Detroit to sell land, and should be back anytime. Now, daughter, how about supper. Your papa's getting hungry after a hard afternoon of play with his grandson."

"It'll be ready soon," she answered, accepting her father's simple explanation, but troubled over the fact that Fenmore would make a business call at the house.

CHAPTER 14

THE FOLLOWING AFTERNOON. Elizabeth sat on the riverbank overlooking the dock, envisioning Jacob's arrival. It seemed good to have some time to herself each day, especially after working hard to grind corn every morning. The warm afternoon sun relaxed her tired muscles, and she soon felt sleepy enough to lean back and close her eyes.

Her dream was the same one she had had for weeks, of Jacob holding her close, pressing his lips to hers, whispering against her hair those precious words, "I love you, Elizabeth." The dream was so real, she was certain he was there with her.

When she opened her eyes, Jacob was staring down at her!

She threw her arms around his neck. "Oh, Jacob, you *are* here," she murmured, "I thought I was dreaming!"

"Elizabeth, I've missed you so," he managed between kisses that showered her face and circled her ear, then trailed down her neck.

"Don't ever leave me again, Jacob. I couldn't bear it."

He held her so close, she could feel his heart thumping against her. "I never want to be without you," he answered. "I've been miserable since the day we parted."

Jacob helped Elizabeth up, and they began walking toward the house. Now that the first intense moments of their reunion had passed, she studied him. "Jacob, you look very tired," she observed, noticing crinkles about his eyes that hadn't been there when he'd left Riverton.

"The trip home was rough. I waited until we reached Upper Saginaw to get off the steamer, since I had business there to take care of."

"Did you see Mr. Fenmore?"

He nodded. "I've just walked the two miles back from there. After a sleepless night, I guess that accounts for my being tired."

"I suppose so," Elizabeth half-agreed, thinking he hadn't given her near enough explanation for the weary-worn look she saw in his face.

"Your father is looking well," he mentioned. "Darius has grown so big, I almost didn't recognize him. And the house never looked better." Though he was saying all the right words, his tone lacked enthusiasm.

"You've been home already?" Elizabeth asked, crestfallen.

"I *did* look for you at the house first," he explained, "and your father told me I'd probably find you by the river."

Her brows lifted in understanding. "Jacob?" She stopped, turning to face him. "Did you sell that farmland?"

A muscle twitched along his jawline before he curled one corner of his mouth upward. "I've just come home after being away for two months—"

"—*more* than two months," she corrected.

"More than two months," he continued, "and my

wife, whom I've missed terribly, and want to shower with my affection, wants to talk business," he teased. "I've had enough business talk for one day. We'll discuss it tomorrow." He pulled her close and kissed her forehead. "Now come on." He started toward home again with his arm about her waist. Turning to her with a broad grin, he added, "I'm in desperate need of one of your homecooked suppers." Jacob half lifted her feet off the ground as he hurried her along, making her laugh.

When they arrived at the house, Elizabeth's father was carrying a feather tick up the stairs.

"Papa, what are you doing?"

"Moving into my bedroom," he answered nonchalantly.

"But Papa, it's not nearly ready," she protested.

He continued up the steps. "It's ready enough, daughter. You and your husband deserve some privacy."

Elizabeth looked questioningly at Jacob. He shrugged, then helped her father move the mattress and frame of his bed while Elizabeth tended to her hearth.

During supper, Jacob refused to answer any questions about Detroit, and instead, insisted Elizabeth tell him everything that had happened in Riverton since he had left.

When supper was finished, Papa shooed Elizabeth and Jacob away from the table. "I'll clean up. You two go off by yourselves."

They walked hand in hand along the river, listening to the breeze rustle through the white pines, and watching the yellow moon rise in the evening sky to illumine ripples on the river as it flowed gently toward Saginaw Bay. For a long time, neither spoke while they held each other close. It was a time of bonding, of renewing their love, and for Elizabeth, of looking toward the days ahead with Jacob by her side.

Later that night, as Elizabeth fell asleep next to Jacob, she knew she would sleep much more soundly than she had since the end of June.

When the morning sun streamed past bedroom curtains, shining on Elizabeth's eyes, she awoke with a start. Most days, she was up at dawn, but today she had overslept, and Darius was crying for her. Still groggy, she reached for her wrapper, then remembered, though the other side of her bed was empty, Jacob was home! She picked up Darius and hurried out of the bedroom to find her husband. Her father was sitting in the common room, reading a letter.

"Good morning, Papa. Have you seen Jacob?"

He looked over the top of his reading glasses, shaking his head. "No, I haven't," he answered slowly folding the letter.

"I suppose wherever he's gone, he'll be back soon for a homecooked breakfast," she concluded. "I'll see to the eggs as soon as I've finished with Darius."

Her father made no response.

Later, when Elizabeth emerged from her bedroom, she rekindled the kitchen fire, and was reaching for a bowl when she noticed a folded paper propped behind the lantern on the mantle. Her name was penned in Jacob's hand on the outside. She opened it and read.

My dearest Elizabeth,

I love you so very much, my beautiful and loving wife, that I hope you will understand it is only with great difficulty that I write this letter.

Because of my love for you, I wanted a good life, a better life than we could have in New York, and for a while, it looked like we had achieved our dream, but my dear one, it is not meant to be.

You asked about the land, and I will tell you. Though I did all I could to sell it and recover my investment, I failed to do so. You can never know, or understand the hardships I endured in Detroit, having run out of funds soon after I arrived. If it weren't for Isaac, I doubt I'd

184

have tried for so long to survive. He gave me the savvy I needed, and the two of us often found odd jobs, earning enough for a bed and a meal, while continuing to seek buyers for our properties.

As you know, Mr. Fenmore holds the mortgage on our house, and I had paid him through August before I left. When I came home yesterday, a day after the September payment was due, I learned he had already come in search of me for the money, and had spoken with your father, who had made the payment for me. I informed Mr. Fenmore that I could no longer afford to live in the house, and had no hopes of finding someone to buy me out, having recently come from Detroit where I had failed to sell unimproved farmland. He suggested that I make arrangements for a loan from your father. I thanked him for the suggestion, and left.

When I returned home, I learned that Uncle Will had been hired to finish the upstairs bedrooms. Though I truly appreciate your father's generous nature, I cannot live off his charity.

Elizabeth, I promised myself once we left that crude cabin, I would never ask you to live like that again, yet that is all I can afford to provide. Seeing the house, and how your father has improved it with his furnishings and his expenditures, I am happy to know that you are finally living in the comfortable surroundings you deserved from the day we came to Riverton.

The truth of the matter is, my dearest, that I own nothing but unimproved land. I have no money, no savings left, not even a Spanish quarter for a pike. It will be years before I recover financial stability. The effects of the banking panic in the East have come to roost in Michigan, and the entire economy is at a standstill. I would never ask you to endure the hardships that I will face, and so leave you with my love, entrusting you and our son to your father's care.

I have written your father a letter also, explaining my desperate straits, my sinful pride in not wanting to accept his charity, and offering him my investment in the house for his own, since he is able to carry the burden of payments, and I am not.

Please do not seek me out, Elizabeth, for I am ashamed that I have not provided better for you, and could not face the humiliation. I beg you to let me bow out gracefully, until the day comes when I can provide for you as you so richly deserve. I am hoping you will wait for that time, but will understand if you are unable to. I will never love anyone but you, my darling, and leaving you and our son now is the most difficult decision I have ever had to make. I promise to return for you as soon as I can.

Love, Jacob.

Elizabeth shook her head, not accepting, not believing that Jacob was gone. Suddenly, she didn't care that he hadn't been able to sell the land, that his investment had been a mistake. What was money, or a fine house without Jacob? Didn't he know that he was more important to her than any possessions? She thought back to the conversation she had had with Mrs. Clarke so long ago, and how at one time she had wondered if she would be able to forgive Jacob if he lost his money. How much she had matured since that day! It didn't matter a bit whether he was penniless, or that he could afford nothing but a cabin, she wanted only to be with him. She must find him, and tell him that! In shock, she went to her father, her letter in hand.

He looked up into her face, his sad eyes drowning in hers. "I'm sorry, Elizabeth, so sorry."

"Papa, I have to find him," her words were a half-whisper.

He nodded.

"Where could he have gone? Did he say anything to you at all?"

Regret showed in the lines of his face as he shook his head. "No, nothing," he answered, then his brows shot up. "Elizabeth, yesterday afternoon, he spent quite a while talking with his uncle before he came to find you. I didn't hear much, only a word now and then, but I'm certain Will knows where he went."

Elizabeth swallowed hard. "Thank you, Papa. Please, can you watch Darius while I go talk to him?"

"Of course. Go."

Elizabeth ran out the door and down the trail, then slowed to a walk as she sorted things out. Usually, Will had already begun working upstairs by this time in the morning, but today he hadn't shown up, probably because he knew Jacob's plan, and couldn't face the awkwardness of the situation.

How could she face Will, though, after all the hard feelings she had harbored against him? *O dear God,* she prayed. *Please help me know what to say.* She hoped he would agree to talk with her, though she couldn't blame him if he wouldn't.

She started running again, and didn't stop until she reached the blockhouse door. She opened it and looked inside. In the dim light, she could barely see, then she noticed the lantern in one corner, and heard Will working there in his workshop. Quietly, she approached him. He was sanding a piece of wood, and didn't look up until she spoke his name.

"Uncle Will, can I talk to you?"

He half-glanced in her direction, then kept on working. "I don't believe we've got much to say to one another, Elizabeth. Least that's the way it's been 'tween you and me for a long time now."

She went straight to the point. "Please, Uncle Will. Do you know where Jacob went?"

He nodded his head.

"Where? You've got to tell me."

"Nope. I can't do that. I gave Jacob my word I'd keep his secret, and I'm not about to make a liar out of myself. My deceit was what got you upset with me in the first place. I'm not about to make that mistake again."

"But Uncle Will, this is different," she urgently insisted. "I've got to see him, got to tell him it doesn't matter that he hasn't any money, that we can only afford to live in a cabin, our love for each other makes up for that. You've got to tell me where I can find him.''

Will stood firm. "No ma'am." He put down his wood and sandpaper and looked her straight in the eye. "You may not believe it, but I've changed, Elizabeth. Back when you told me I was putting profit ahead of honesty, I brushed it off. I liked money too much to worry how I came by it. Going near broke when the bank folded did something to me. All at once, I realized that it isn't money that's important in this world at all, it's what you can't buy with money that has meaning to it.''

"Then you know why I've got to find Jacob.''

Will took a deep breath, stroked his beard thoughtfully, then spoke. "All right, tell you what. You go on home for a while. I'll go talk with Jacob, tell him what you said, and try to make him understand, but I don't have much hope he'll listen. I doubt he's ready to come back and face up to his circumstances. I spent a good long time yesterday afternoon tryin' to explain to him that money wasn't as important as he was makin' it out to be, but he wouldn't pay any attention.''

"I'd appreciate your trying, Will. Thank you.'' Awkwardly, Elizabeth moved toward him, and on impulse, hugged his neck. Will stiffened slightly, then returned her hug. She started to leave, then turned back. "I want to tell you how sorry I am that your bank failed.''

"Thank you, Elizabeth.''

Hesitantly, she continued. "Can you forgive me for my angry outbursts last fall? I shouldn't have spoken so harshly to you.''

A moment passed before he nodded. "You're forgiven. And Elizabeth . . . please forgive me for what I did. I see a different side to things now.''

"With all my heart, Uncle Will. I've learned a few things, too.''

As Elizabeth turned to go, she saw Louisa silhouetted in the doorway. Louisa dipped her head as she turned and hurried away. Elizabeth ran after her. "Louisa, wait! I want to talk to you!" The woman stopped on the path. When Elizabeth reached her, they exchanged awkward glances, and Elizabeth noticed the careworn look on her neighbor's face. Haltingly, Elizabeth spoke. "Louisa, . . . I'm sorry."

"Elizabeth, I'm sorry, too," Louisa interrupted, biting nervously on her lower lip.

Elizabeth reached out her hand. "Friends?"

Louisa nodded, placing her hand in Elizabeth's. "Friends." She hugged Elizabeth tightly.

Seconds later, they parted. Elizabeth gestured in the direction of her home. "I have to get back."

"I know." Louisa nodded in understanding.

"But we'll have coffee sometime," Elizabeth added.

Louisa's mouth curved into a tiny smile. "I'd like that."

"See you later, Louisa." Elizabeth waved, then hurried along the riverbank toward home.

Elizabeth waited and waited, but Jacob didn't return home that day, nor did Will come to work on the upstairs bedroom the following morning. Time dragged by, and she was glad to have her garden vegetables to put up, but try as she may, she could not get her mind off what had happened. Two days later, Will stopped by to talk with her.

"Elizabeth, you're just going to have to be patient. Jacob's going through a very rough time."

"Did you tell him I'd live anywhere with him? That it makes no difference to me, as long as we're together?"

Will nodded. "I told him you could have Louisa's cabin, but he's worried that, even if the three of you lived in a borrowed cabin, he couldn't provide enough food to keep you from starving through the winter."

"But we have plenty," she countered, then hurried to the pantry to fill a macock, a birch bark container Beloved-of-the-Forest had given her, with dried vegetables. "Here. Take him this, and tell him that while he was gone, I grew a garden, and put up enough corn, beans, and squash to see us through until spring."

Will took the container. "I'll tell him, but he's feeling so bad about himself, it's like he won't pay any attention to what I say to him. He just keeps mumbling about your being better off without him, now that your papa's here to take good care of you."

Elizabeth thought for a moment, then responded. "Uncle Will, I'm going to take you up on your offer of Louisa's cabin. Starting right now, Darius and I are moving out of this house. I'm taking only what Jacob and I own, nothing more. You have to convince him how much I need him to chop the wood, to snare the rabbits, to catch and clean the fish. You tell him that when he's ready again, his son and I will be waiting for him at Louisa's cabin."

Jacob lay in the corner of the defunct Riverton Bank on a pile of hemlock boughs. He had eaten very little since the homecooked supper Elizabeth had made him, but it didn't matter, he wasn't hungry anyway. He hated what he had become; a shadow of the man he had been the day he left Riverton to sell his land in Detroit. The hardships in the city had worn him down, but more than anything, he had felt worthless once he had returned to Riverton and realized he had been replaced as a provider for his wife and child.

He held no bitterness toward Elizabeth's father. In fact, the opposite was true, he was thankful for his father-in-law's intervention. At least Elizabeth and Darius were comfortable, without wants, and far better off than if Papa Brownell had not come to live in Riverton.

Jacob felt like a defeated man, someone who had taken on life's challenges and been beaten down by them. He had made mistakes, bad choices, and had no right to ask his wife to pay for them.

Sometimes it scared Jacob that he really didn't care whether he ever dragged himself up from the depths of his despair. His letter to Elizabeth had been a noble gesture, but he didn't know if he would ever see the day when he could go back to her and his son with his head held high. He had torn himself away from her after one night because he was afraid of what his failure would do the three of them.

He loved his wife, cherished their son, but had repressed those feelings to keep himself from going back to them. Now, after reminding himself for hours on end how much happier they were without him there to pull them down, he didn't even care much for life anymore.

A coded knock, two quick taps, a pause, then a third tap signified that Will had come to see him again, and Jacob mustered enough energy to remove the bolt, then flop back down on his hemlock mattress.

Will stepped inside and bolted the door again, then sat on a stump chair.

"Here," he said, dropping the macock at Jacob's feet. "Elizabeth sends her love."

Jacob removed the lid. In the dim light, it was hard to see what was inside the container. "What's this? It looks like corn kernels," he commented, turning several over in the palm of his hand.

Jacob crunched on a kernel, then tossed several more into his mouth. The toasted flavor appealed to him, though he had thought his appetite had left him.

Will spoke. "Elizabeth's put up enough to last until next spring. She grew a garden this summer and dried her vegetables."

Jacob wanted to ask more about his wife and child, but restrained himself from doing so.

"When are you going to stop feeling sorry for yourself, and go back to your wife? You were a fool to leave her, Jacob. Why, a woman like Elizabeth would be appealing to any man, and she's going to need a man around, now that she's moved into Louisa's cabin."

Jealousy stirred in Jacob, then he caught on to his uncle's ploy. "I don't believe you. You're just trying to trick me. Why would she give up a comfortable house for that drafty box you call a cabin?"

"Because she loves you, and she wants you back, and she knows you've got too much pride to live off her pa. Elizabeth just wants to be with you, Jacob, under *any* circumstances. Can't you accept that?"

He shook his head vigorously. "No! I'm not going back until I can go back with dignity. That means with money. I can wait a long time for that day to come, if I have to."

"You're the most bullheaded man I've ever known, Jacob Morgan! You think it was easy for me, when my bank failed, and my sawmill went to Fenmore? You think it didn't hurt my dignity when I had to take a job doing carpentry work for Elizabeth's father? Why, I'd been on the hiring end just months before!" Will laughed derisively. "Money means nothing compared to the love of a good woman. You're too blind to see that, just like I was. You can't see past your own selfishness. Well, that's too bad, because your wife needs you. A woman can't survive in that cabin without a man around to take care of things, and she's bound and determined to stay in that drafty box, so you'd better give some serious thought to going back and helping her out. Don't think I'm going to step in for you and take over 'cause I won't. I've got responsibilities of my own. Far as I'm concerned, that wife and son of yours can just sit in that place and freeze unless you get a move on and start chopping wood."

Jacob remained silent.

"Elizabeth's a strong lady, Jacob, but she can't survive without you. She knows it, and I think you know it. Now what are you going to do about it?"

Will's stare bored hard into Jacob, then he let himself out, pulling the door shut behind him with an extra hard thud. Jacob shuddered in the fear of his self-imposed solitude.

As Elizabeth stored away her dried vegetables, she thought back to the day she had visited Beloved-of-the-Forest. Then, she couldn't imagine herself growing a garden. She had planted it to please others, tended it out of a need to fill the long, lonely hours while Jacob was away, and preserved the harvest to satisfy the concerns of her Chippewa friend. She never could have believed that she would actually come to depend on the results of her efforts for life-giving nourishment.

Her next task was to hang the curtains from the frame house at the cabin window. At least, if she was going to live in the small, crude structure, she would make it as pleasant an experience as possible. Besides, the curtains were paid for by Jacob, not her father, so she was well within her rights to keep them.

It was a challenge to keep her eye on Darius while tending to the outdoor chores, such as hauling water, and chopping wood for the cooking fire. Her infant was a strong crawler and needed constant attention. How much easier her life would be when Jacob returned, and she was certain he would, any day now. Will had assured her that he impressed on Jacob how much she needed his help to survive. Surely he wouldn't let her struggle alone for long.

September weather brought mild and warm days, with chilly autumn nights. Day after day, Elizabeth prayed for Jacob's return, yet found herself alone in the feather bed each night.

The month had been unusually dry, and when black storm clouds gathered overhead one day near the end of the month, Elizabeth feared that she and Darius were in for severe weather. She listened to the rumblings, at first distant, grow louder as the thunder clouds rolled in. The wind whipped up, gusting through the pines, and Elizabeth bolted the shutters closed on the only window, making the interior of the cabin even darker than usual. As the first drops of rain started to fall, she gathered an extra armload of firewood and brought it inside, stacking it next to the hearth of the stick-and-mud chimney. A few fat raindrops spattered against the parched ground, hurrying her toward the well to fill a second bucket with water, in case the storm should be a long one.

She was just lifting the bucket from the well when a streak of lightning, so bright it almost blinded her, bolted from the sky, crackling as it snapped at her chimney. She froze in horror as flames licked at the dry sticks which were embedded in the chimney mud, working their way quickly toward the cabin roof. Elizabeth dropped her pail and ran.

When she reached the cabin, thick smoke already filled the air. "Darius!" she screamed. *Please Lord, help me find my baby*, she prayed. Her eyes and throat burned as she groped through the poisonous haze, feeling her way. "Darius, cry!" she begged, "Help Mama find you!" She dropped to her knees, where the air was clearer, and crawled along the puncheon floor toward the back of the cabin.

Suddenly, a familiar strong arm went around her waist, lifting her off the floor, pinning her tightly against a hipbone. Jacob's voice was reassuring as he carried her toward the door, "He's safe. I have him."

Outside, Jacob set her gently on her feet. She looked up into his face, and thought the worry lines had never seemed more handsome. "Thank God, you came in time, Jacob," were the only words she could say before her throat closed tight, knotted with relief that her son was safe, and her husband had returned.

Holding his son close, Jacob wrapped one arm about her waist, pulling her snuggly against him, kissing the raindrops from her face as quickly as they fell. Crackling wood drew their eyes to the cabin, which was soon engulfed in flames. Jacob held her tightly. "Elizabeth, I was a fool to leave you, and an even bigger fool to let my pride get in the way. I never should have turned my back on your father's help. It almost cost me my son and my wife. Can you ever forgive me for all the hurt my pride has caused you?"

"Jacob, I love you so much, of course I'll forgive you, but you must make me a promise." She ran a finger over his brow with a smile smoothing away his worry.

"All you need to do is ask." He kissed her forehead again and again.

She spoke in a whisper. "Jacob, you must promise never to leave us again."

"Elizabeth, my love, I give you promises from my heart. I'll always stay by your side, and I'll always love you." And she knew that those words were true. The man she had always loved and believed in had come home to her. For good.

Louisa's tiny cabin burned to the ground that day. Elizabeth knew in her heart the reason why. God had used the crude dwelling to serve many purposes, and now he used its destruction to serve another. Jacob moved with Elizabeth and Darius into the frame house and never wasted another moment in self-pity over his failures.

In the months to come, Elizabeth and Jacob renewed their bonds of love. Though years would pass before Jacob regained his former financial status, Elizabeth didn't mind, for though they were often poor of cash, they were always rich in love.

ABOUT THE AUTHOR

DONNA WINTERS loves to explore history. With her husband, Fred, who has taught American History for fifteen years, she enjoys visiting various restored villages and historic sites. "We go with our tape recorder and camera loaded, trying to capture a slice of America's past which I can share with my readers or Fred can share with his students."

Donna and Fred live in a small midwestern farming village, a town so small they can walk their dog around the entire community in less than an hour every night. "I love a slow pace and quiet life," she explains. "It's perfect for creating romances."

A Letter to Our Readers

Dear Reader:

Welcome to the world of Serenade Books—a series designed to bring you the most beautiful love stories in the world of inspirational romance. They will uplift you, encourage you, and provide hours of wholesome entertainment, so thousands of readers have testified. In order that we might better contribute to your reading enjoyment, we would appreciate your taking a few minutes to respond to the following questions and return to:

> Editor, Serenade Books
> The Zondervan Publishing House
> 1415 Lake Drive, S.E.
> Grand Rapids, Michigan 49506

1. Did you enjoy reading ELIZABETH OF SAGINAW BAY?

   ☐ Very much. I would like to see more books by this author!
   ☐ Moderately
   ☐ I would have enjoyed it more if _____

   _____

2. Where did you purchase this book? _____

3. What influenced your decision to purchase this book?
   ☐ Cover   ☐ Back cover copy
   ☐ Title   ☐ Friends
   ☐ Publicity   ☐ Other _____

4. What are some inspirational themes you would like to see treated in future books?

_____

5. Please indicate your age range:
   - [ ] Under 18
   - [ ] 18–24
   - [ ] 25–34
   - [ ] 35–45
   - [ ] 46–55
   - [ ] Over 55

6. If you are interested in receiving information about our Serenade Home Reader Service, in which you will be offered new and exciting novels on a regular basis, please give us your name and address. (This does NOT obligate you for membership.)

Name _____

Occupation _____

Address _____

City _____ State _____ Zip _____

Serenade / Saga books are inspirational romances in historical settings, designed to bring you a joyful, heart-lifting reading experience.

Serenade / Saga books available in your local book store:

Serenade / Serenata books are inspirational romances in contemporary settings, designed to bring you a joyful, heart-lifting reading experience.

Serenade / Serenata books available in your local bookstore:

Watch for other books in both the *Serenade/Saga* (historical) and *Serenade/Serenata* (contemporary) series coming soon.